A SEASON FOR EVERYTHING
BEVERLY VARNADO

A SEASON FOR EVERYTHING by BEVERLY VARNADO

ANAIAH SEASONAL
An imprint of ANAIAH PRESS, LLC.
7780 49th ST N. #129
Pinellas Park, FL 33781

A Season for Everything copyright © 2020 Beverly Varnado

First Anaiah Seasonal print edition November 2020

Edited by Kara Leigh Miller
Book Design by Anaiah Press
Cover Design by Laura Heritage

ISBN 978-1-947327-96-2

Anaiah Press
Books that Inspire

With much love and gratitude to my dear lifelong mentors and friends, Rev. Grady and Doris Wigley.

"I thank my God every time I remember you" (Philippians 1:3).

ACKNOWLEDGEMENTS

Special thanks to my husband, Jerry, who encouraged me as I finished writing *A Season for Everything* during the Corona quarantine. You are a blessing beyond words. As always, thank you for the legal advice to my characters.

Many thanks also to others in my precious family, Aaron, Bethany, Mari, Brent, Walker, Sara Alden, Tammy, Foy, and Christopher. One day soon, we will all be together and share hugs and kisses.

I continue to honor my lifelong spiritual mentors, Dr. Warren and Jane Lathem, Dr. Gary and Diane Whetstone, Rev. Walton and Martha McNeal, and especially Rev. Grady and Doris Wigley to whom this book is dedicated.

Many blessings to my readers at my blog, One Ringing Bell. Thank you for the gift of your precious time.

To my writing group friends. So thankful for our mutual encouragement to each other in our writing pursuits.

Remembering always with love my mom and dad.

ONE

Catherine Todd cruised down the state highway, which turned into Main Street closer to the little town of Worthville. On this unseasonably warm December day, she decided to do a little Christmas shopping.

As she neared the city limits and rounded a curve, a sleek white convertible with the top down emerged from Betty's Bed and Breakfast and pulled out right in front of her. She slammed on the breaks and blew the horn.

The driver in the red baseball cap and striped red shirt threw up his hand. He hit the gas, pulling away from her at lightning speed, but not before she caught sight of the vanity license plate—BRDSRUS.

"Reckless tourist," Catherine called after him, adrenaline spiking in her.

More and more people were coming to Worthville to visit the old mill and take in the

1

small-town charm, including the centerpiece of the town—the restored train depot—which often functioned as the town's art gallery. Most of the tourists, however, were gentle folk who didn't come close to causing accidents.

As the car disappeared in the distance, she tried to tamp down her anger. She wouldn't let someone's selfishness take away from what she hoped would be a lighthearted day. Wasn't Christmas shopping supposed to be fun? Especially when shopping for children. She was desperate for Christmas this year to be different from the most recent ones. Oh, how she hoped to actually enjoy the holiday rather than just try to get through it.

She rolled into town alongside the garland-wrapped gaslights that were also festooned with red bows and bells. She found a parking spot next to Harry's Hardware, exited her SUV, and checked the evergreen and twinkle light trimmed front window. Four weeks from December 25th, and it seemed everyone in town was ready for Christmas, except her. A plaid-ribbon-bedecked blue bicycle just John's size dominated the Christmas display. *Perfect. It's still here.*

She pushed on the old wooden entrance door that sported a colorful wreath and entered the store, which smelled of an odd mixture of paint fumes and cinnamon.

"Catherine," Alexander Steuben called her name from his place at the freshly painted counter, on top of which sat a small Christmas tree. He gave his Harry's Hardware cap a twist for emphasis as he often did. "May we help you with your shopping?"

Alexander owned the store. One of the things she loved about Worthville was the alliterative store names, which sometimes had nothing to do with the actual proprietor's moniker.

"As a matter of fact, you can." She pointed toward the window. "I'd like that blue bicycle for John. He's been asking for it. Could I purchase it and then you hold it until Christmas? I don't have a place to store it."

"Right away," he said. Alexander strode to the window and started to attach a sold tag to the bike. "Oh, no."

Never good words to hear around Christmas. "What is it?" Catherine asked, her throat tightening.

"There's already a tag on the bicycle. See." He held a ticket attached to one of the spokes with a big bold S-O-L-D. "I am sorry. Isabelle must have made the sale while I was at lunch."

"Is there another one in the back?"

"Not in blue. This is our last one. Been a good seller this year."

Catherine sighed. "What about a special order?"

3

"I could, but it wouldn't be here until after Christmas. It takes a while to get these shipped in. I'm guessing that wouldn't work for you." Alexander returned to the counter.

Catherine stared down at her empty hands. "Thanks anyway." Her chest ached.

This was her fault. She turned and shuffled to the front door. Why hadn't she come in sooner? She knew why. For as much progress as she'd made dealing with her grief these past two years, something about Christmas seemed to bring it back full force. This would be their third Christmas since the deaths. Shopping seemed as hard this year as it had the first year. She'd kept putting it off.

A cheery "Merry Christmas" door sign seemed to mock her as she made her exit. When she reached the sidewalk, an idea hit her. She pivoted and ran back in. "You said there wasn't a blue one. Do you have the same bike in other colors?"

"Yes, but . . ."

"Maybe the other person would be willing to take another color?'

Alexander raised an eyebrow. "I don't know . . ."

"Please? This is all John has asked for, and it's my fault for not coming in sooner."

"I guess I could ask . . ."

Catherine ran around the counter and hugged Alexander. "Thank you very much."

She left the store, more hopeful, and strode over to Tucker's Tomes to buy a book the kids wanted—a children's picture book on birds with gorgeous illustrations. She'd seen it online, but she liked to give Tucker the business.

As she pushed on the door to enter, a sign announcing a book signing with the author of the bird book grabbed her attention. *Georgia Birds and Their Stories* by Collin Donnelly, she read. The date was for the upcoming Saturday. *Hmm . . . might be something fun to do this time of year.* Maybe she'd buy the book now and come back on Saturday with the kids so they could meet the author. That could boost their spirits.

She entered the store. Tucker stood at the counter, his bright red shirt a stark contrast to his dark skin. He was helping a man who said, "Tucker, you've saved me. I would have never thought of this book for Dahlia without you." Tucker extended his hand. The man shook it.

"Tell her I hope she enjoys it," Tucker said in his magnetic voice.

On one end of Tucker's store window, he'd created an amazing Christmas tree of books, which he'd layered and draped with lights. On the other end, his signature revolving light up globe lent a festive air no matter what season it was. Between them, he'd created a display of children's books, including the one her kids wanted. She plucked a book from the window and took a moment to browse through it. As she did, a cell phone rang from the stacks behind her.

"Hi, Alexander." A pause. "Would I consider a color other than blue? I don't know. I'm not sure my nephew wants or needs a bike, but this purchase does help me finish my shopping."

Catherine closed the book and edged closer to the voice behind her.

"You know I'm the kind of uncle who likes to buy his way into children's hearts. Tell the other person to pick something else. The bike is sold."

Catherine could see herself as one of those cartoon characters drawn with steam coming from their ears.

Tucker strolled to the stack behind her and said in his commanding voice, "Collin, we're looking forward to the book signing."

"Right. I am, too," the same voice said. "The children's book has done well."

Collin? Children's book? She glanced at the book in her hand and reread the author's name—Collin Donnelly. She crept around the end of the shelves and peered at the speaker. It couldn't be. Red and white striped shirt. Red baseball cap.

"It's you," she said. *"The reckless tourist."*

He spun around. "I'm sorry. I don't think I understand."

"You almost caused me to have an accident, and then you buy my son's bicycle." Catherine turned and headed toward the door, leaving the book on the counter.

Once outside, she strode to her vehicle, got in, and turned toward home. She passed Betty's Bed and Breakfast, her knuckles white on the steering wheel.

However, the closer she got to home, the more she regretted her outburst. It was not like her. Not like her at all. Some people used to say she was absurdly optimistic. Well, they said that until two and a half years ago.

She pulled into the driveway at home, rested her head on the steering wheel, and whispered a prayer, "God, please help me. I am weary of the way I am."

TWO

Catherine exited the car, crossed the road, knocked on her neighbor's front door, and peeked around the garland through the sidelights. Genny Sanders-Worth approached in slow motion, her enormous belly leading the way. Being seven and one-half months pregnant with twins, a boy and a girl, slowed her down in a big way.

As Catherine waited, Genny's pet hen Elizabeth strutted across the porch, giving her customary cluck as a greeting.

She bent over and gave the hen a stroke on the head. "Hi to you, too, Elizabeth. Glad to see you looking well."

She couldn't put her finger on it, but something about Genny's hen, Elizabeth, was so consoling. The most unusual of pets, she was as devoted to Genny as she was to Genny's grandmother, Agnes, before her passing. Catherine missed Agnes, but what a blessing to have her granddaughter, Genny, living in this house.

Genny opened the door and motioned for her to come in. "Catherine, good to see you. Come in and have a seat. Oh, Elizabeth, I need to feed you. Hold on." Genny turned to waddle back to the kitchen.

"I'll feed Elizabeth," Catherine said. "You have a seat." Catherine strode to the laundry room where Genny kept the poultry feed in a large plastic container. She scooped a serving, went down the stairs in the back, and cast it into the yard. Elizabeth came running at the sound of the screen door slamming.

Catherine returned to the living room where Genny had lowered herself into a wing chair. Catherine searched for a place to sit as she scanned the sofa and armchair full of books, magazines, and newspapers.

Genny gestured to the furniture. "Okay, push something over. House cleaning has moved down on my to-do list these days."

Catherine stacked a few books and took a seat on the sofa, "So are you still working at Dr. Fleming's?"

"I'm trying to as long as I can because we're so busy."

Catherine moved a throw pillow behind her. "I guess your absence would leave a big hole. Surely, he has someone else coming to cover for you?"

Genny nodded. "He's hired another nurse practitioner who's arriving soon, but I'm still trying to hang on for half days at least." She sighed and leaned her head against the back of the chair. "Anyway, when I get home, I'm exhausted. David's legal practice has taken off, so he's been slammed at work with extra hours and trying to oversee the happenings at the mill. He's attempting to finish up his work before the babies come."

"You need to take care of yourself . . ." She paused. Should she go on with the reason she came?

But, as if reading her mind, Genny said, "What's with you?"

Catherine leveled her gaze at Genny. "You know the part in the Bible that says, "Confess your sins one to another . . .?"

Genny nodded.

"Well, Dr. Sanders-Worth, I'm here to confess."

"Tell me everything."

Catherine went through the almost accident and the bicycle business. "And then I let Collin Donnelly have it right there in Tucker's Tomes. In front of God and everybody. I'm so embarrassed."

Genny studied her a moment. "You know, Catherine," she said and paused again, appearing to ponder her next words. "There are many stages to grief. They don't always come in the same order, and it's not as if you work through one and check it off the list. Sometimes, it returns. Anger is one of the stages, and it can manifest in strange ways."

Catherine slumped. "I know. I've read much about grief stages. Denial, anger, bargaining, depression, and acceptance," she recited. "I think I've covered them all. Well, except the acceptance part. I'm not there. I still have days when I think Don will walk in the door at five o'clock." She let go a big breath of air and fell back against the chair. She'd be standing in the kitchen, hear the clock in the hallway chime, and just know she'd soon hear the crunch of gravel in the driveway. The sense of longing for Don almost overwhelmed her at times.

"And . . ." Genny continued. "You lost your dad six months after that. It had to feel as if the whole world was ripped from under you."

Catherine nodded. "Exactly." Her dad used to call every night at 9 o'clock. If her phone rang in the evening, she still half expected it to be him.

"And I'm guessing Christmas has a way of multiplying the grief." Genny grimaced a little as she shifted in her seat. "I know after my grandmother passed, I struggled around Christmastime. All the memories and wishing you could have them back for even a minute or two."

11

"It does, for sure." Catherine fiddled with the fringe on a throw next to her. "But, I was praying this morning about how tired I am of being this way. On the one hand, I'm still not at acceptance, but on the other, my frustration at how stuck I am is growing. I guess that's good."

"I'm sure it is, and I know God hears your prayers." Genny leaned forward and extended her hands. "Remember, many are praying for you, including me and David."

"I know, and I appreciate it. Back to matters at hand . . . I have to apologize. No matter if he did steal my son's bike and almost made me wreck." If she were being any kind of reasonable person, she needed to give him the benefit of the doubt that both of those incidences were unintentional.

Catherine grew quiet again, wondering whether to mention something else she'd been pondering.

"What else?" Genny asked

"I've been thinking of going back to work. After Don's death, I wanted to be available to the kids, and, since he was such a good financial planner, I was able to be there for them, but the kids are both in school and doing well. I think it's time."

Genny pulled on what Catherine believed to be a denim shirt that belonged to David, trying to make it cover her protrusion. Genny still had six weeks to go, and Catherine wasn't sure David's wardrobe would go the distance.

"Sounds good. What are the opportunities in Worthville?" Genny asked.

"Well, not many. And I can't move. The kids' lives have been disrupted so much already. I don't know what my business degree might lend itself to here, or if I even have what it takes. People I graduated from school with are working for huge corporations. I'll be starting all over."

"I know it will be hard, but I'm sure you can do it. I have faith in you," Genny said in affirmation. Then, a coy smiled eased across her face. "Was he cute?"

"Was who cute?"

"The reckless tourist . . . the book author . . . the bicycle stealer?"

Catherine thought a minute. "Yes, I guess he was, but Genny, I'm not ready."

"I get it. I heard what you said. But you don't know when you will be. Best to keep your options open."

Catherine shook her head. "Even if I was ready, that convertible driving Collin Donnelly would not be my choice." She stood. "Thanks for listening." A Christmas tree occupied a corner with ornaments sparsely scattered on it and open boxes sitting at its base. "Not finished decorating, huh?"

"I know most people go through a nesting phase before they have a baby, but I'm too tired to nest."

Catherine pointed to the coffee table, which held the remains of something brown, red, and unrecognizable on a plate. "May I take that plate back to the kitchen for you?' she asked as she lifted it and tried to decipher its identity. "What was it?"

"Toast with smashed bananas and jalapenos."

Catherine winced. "You ate that?"

"Why, yes. It was delicious."

Catherine decided to clear out before Genny offered her a snack made from her pregnancy craving menu. "I'll take this to the kitchen. Thanks for listening. I have to go."

"I'll see you out." Genny tried her best to rise from the chair. But after heaving herself up a couple of times without success, she rolled her eyes at Catherine. "Know anyone with a crane?"

Catherine entered Worthville Elementary around lunch the next day—her turn to volunteer in the library. She always enjoyed her shifts meeting the children and helping them select a book. She studied a poster on the library window. "Worthville Elementary is proud to announce our Author in Residence for a day—Collin Donnelly."

Nooooo. She peered through the window, and there he sat, reading, holding the children's attention better than any video game could. She glanced around. Maybe no one saw her enter, and she could back up and call in sick. She scrunched up, trying to make herself smaller, and let her hair fall over her face. Then she took a step back and then another. *Oh, if I can just get out of here.*

The media specialist, Ellen Norwood emerged from thin air. "Catherine, I'm glad this is your day to volunteer. You're going to love Collin Donnelly. He's amazing with the kids." Ellen took her hand and led her into the library, making her feel as if she were going to the gallows. Ellen stopped short. "Doesn't he have the most animated voice? He would be a great voice over artist." She held her finger to her lips. "Let's listen."

Catherine nodded and feigned a smile, wishing for a trap door to open beneath her. Collin did the voice of a pileated woodpecker named Otis. "Who's been pecking on my tree?" he said in a deep raspy tone.

The children laughed, and Collin glanced away from his book. When he did, his gaze landed on her, and she gave him a weak wave. *Busted. No escaping.*

He held a game face, not letting on that anything passed between them. He waved back.

15

"Do you know him?" Ellen asked. "You waved."

"Know him? I wouldn't say . . ."

Collin continued to read, and in a few moments, he said, "The end," with a flourish. He closed the book and stood.

"Oh, look, he's finished," Ellen said. "Would you mind escorting him to the front door? This is his last class for the day. He's been busy reading all morning. And really, we don't have anything for you to do because he's been here today, so you're free to go."

Catherine flinched as Ellen walked away, dreading the task worse than anything. She would have rather stayed and shelved ten carts of books, dusted the entire nonfiction section, and straightened the stacks after messy kindergartners than be Collin Donnelly's tour guide.

Ellen brought Collin to her. "Collin, this is Catherine, a volunteer here, but I think you may know her already."

Collin nodded. "We've met." He smiled broadly.

"Nice to see you again," Catherine said, sure her face burned a bright red. She moved her foot back and forth on an invisible spot on the floor.

"She'll see you to the door, and thank you again for coming. Our children have enjoyed your visit. I understand you have a book signing at Tucker's.

16

Count on seeing me there," Ellen said, effervescent with enthusiasm.

"I'll look forward to it," he said.

Catherine pointed toward the door. "This way." When they were in the hallway, Catherine used a hushed tone, "I didn't know you were going to be here today. This is awkward."

Collin smiled, appearing amused. "Awkward. Why would you say that?" He chuckled.

"You know why. My outburst yesterday at Tucker's. I shouldn't have spoken to you like that. There's no excuse for my behavior."

Collin grinned. "You'll be happy to know I called my sister, and she said my nephew already has a bike he never rides. If he got a new one, it would be two bikes he never rides. I informed Alexander, and the bike is on hold for you. Also, about pulling in front of you—have you ever exited from Betty's Bed and Breakfast? You can't see a thing around that corner."

Catherine nodded. "I don't know what to say. It's kind of you to make the effort about the bike. And no, I haven't ever exited from Betty's before." She dropped her chin as shame washed over her.

"Forget it, but if you want to make it up to me, let's have coffee . . . I think I saw a place."

Catherine smiled and lifted her head. "Connie's Coffee and Cones. My kids love it there." The truth was, she did, too. "And you have to walk around the corner to Connie's Catering and Confections. Connie's baked goods are unbelievable." She pointed toward the front door, and he followed her.

"I'll do that. How old are your kids?"

"Seven-year-old Lauren, and six-year-old John. You probably read to them, today. My, uh, husband . . . he passed away two and a half years ago." It never seemed easy to say those words.

Collin nodded. "Tucker told me. I'm sorry. Must be hard with such small kids. Tucker also mentioned your dad died a short time later." He held the door open for her.

"It is hard." She hadn't mentioned her dad because it seemed too much to say. She often felt she was heaving a burden onto others when she told them about her losses. "You know, I tend to see the world through the kids' eyes, through their loss."

"And yet, you've suffered a huge loss, too."

She nodded, a mist forming in her eyes. She shook it off. "I'm parked over there. I'll meet you at Connie's." She pointed her feet toward the car, hoping he hadn't seen the moisture. She didn't want to share much of that part of her life with a stranger.

Since Worthville Elementary was within walking distance of town, it didn't take but two minutes to reach the shop. She found a parking space sooner than Collin did, and when she entered, the scent of freshly baked blackberry muffins hit her. All of Connie's muffins were good, but she remembered the first day Connie baked the blackberry ones, and they had been her favorite ever since. Blackberry muffins were one of her biggest consolations. Most of Connie's baked goods were sold through the adjoining bakery and catering shop, but she made sure to have plenty of muffins for the coffee drinkers.

A new plaque on the wall embellished with red berries and holly read, "To everything there is a season, and a time to every purpose under the heaven . . . Ecclesiastes 3:1." Connie often added to her décor of wise sayings and scripture verses.

Catherine liked the verse, but the reality was, some seasons seemed to never end.

"Whoa, I like this place," Collin said glancing around. "Smells like heaven."

She nodded. "It does."

Many a time, Connie's Coffee and Cones had been a refuge for her since Don died. At Christmas, Connie made sure her décor reflected the holiday with a tiny Christmas tree on every table, old fashioned multi-colored lights in the window, and holiday inspired ice cream and coffee flavors.

"Catherine, who's your friend?" She turned to see Connie with her curly blonde hair and infectious smile standing behind the counter.

"This is Collin Donnelly. He was the author in residence at Worthville Elementary this morning."

Connie stuck her hand over the counter. "Pleased to meet you Collin. Connie Cole."

"Oh, wow, I hadn't realized until this moment how much your married name works with your store name," Catherine said.

"An added bonus." Connie grinned. "What will y'all have?"

"I think I'm going to try the peppermint mocha latte," he said.

"Sounds good. Same for me." She retrieved her wallet from her purse to pay.

Collin put his hand out. "No, no, this is on me. The least I can do for almost killing you and nearly destroying your Christmas."

They both laughed and took a seat while waiting for their lattes.

"Just before you went airborne, I read your license plate. BRDSRUS. What do those letters mean?"

He shifted a napkin dispenser on the table to one side. "Sorry about the airborne. Living in Atlanta tends to make you an aggressive driver. I forgot where I was. Yes, birds are us. The short answer is it's what I do. I study birds—to paint and write about, and other reasons."

"Interesting. What's the long answer?"

He opened his mouth, but Connie interrupted as she deposited their lattes on the table and winked at her. Catherine tried not to notice.

"Y'all might want to let those cool a minute cause they're piping hot. Let me know if you need anything else, okay? And Catherine, you have to tell the kids about my new flavor. Christmas Crunch." Again, a wink.

It so distracted Catherine that she forgot her question. "I'll be sure to tell them." She directed her attention to Collin as Connie walked away. She shook her head. "What was I saying? Oh, the long answer. About your interest in birds?"

"I want to make people care. Bird populations have plummeted since the 1970s. Almost thirty percent have disappeared—equating to about three billion birds lost in fifty years."

Those numbers made her cringe. "I read that somewhere. Those are terrible statistics."

"Right, and birds add so much to our world. I love trying to save beautiful things."

Save things. That lovely thought resonated deeply within her. "I do what I can, too." She put her shoulders back and expanded her chest. "I feel somewhat responsible for a whole flock of bluebirds in our area. There weren't many when we first moved to our house, but I hung two bluebird boxes. Generations of birds have lived in them."

21

Now, Collin was winking and giving her a thumbs up. Only his wink had an entirely different effect on her. Her heart rate quickened a bit "Bluebirds are one of the few bird populations increasing. Thanks for being part of that. So . . ." He narrowed his eyes. "Why are you interested in birds?"

He waited on her answer as if he really wanted to hear her response. She paused, wondering how long it'd been since she'd shared this part of her life. "It was my dad. He was an amateur ornithologist. No degree, but lots of autodidactic learning that he loved to pass on to me." She smiled at the happy memory. "We used to have something called the first bird contest when I was little. We'd fill the feeder and then keep a record of the first bird to visit every morning. It's how I learned the bird names and learned to distinguish male from female."

"We need more people like your dad . . . and you."

His comment both pulled her to him, because receiving a compliment like this was nice, but it also made her want to push back from him because hadn't she just told Genny she wasn't ready for a romantic relationship? She glanced up to see Connie giving her a coy smile. Oh, the joy of small town living where everyone wanted to run a person's life. Though, she had to admit, most of the time with Connie, people didn't seem to mind it much.

She directed her attention back to Collin. "How long are you in town?"

"I'm here tomorrow for a book signing at Tucker's, and on Sunday, I'm doing a little bird watching and taking reference photographs. Worthville and its surrounds are resplendent with winter birds." He glanced at the coffee cups. "Do you think they've cooled?"

They both reached for a cup and chose the same one. Their fingers overlapped, and they laughed, but something, and Catherine couldn't say what, something about that incidental happening made her feel like she wasn't half dead from grief anymore.

At least for one fraction of a second.

THREE

On Saturday morning, Catherine refilled her three bird feeders with black-oiled sunflower seeds. That should make the cardinals, chickadees, house finches, wrens, and blue jays happy, not to mention a few squirrels who were too lazy to hide their acorns last summer. From a tree behind her, a cardinal seemed to chirp in gratitude.

"You're welcome," she called to him. She went inside to wrangle the kids for the book signing.

"What's a book signing?" John asked, his brow furrowed.

"You remember the man who read to you yesterday at school, Mr. Donnelly? Well, he's going to be selling his book at Tucker's, and he'll write his name in it."

"But why does he put his name in the book if I'm the one it will belong to?" John asked.

"He signs it because he wrote it, and that makes the book even more special." She tried to smooth John's hair down. One sprig always stuck straight up.

"Is it kind of like when we sign the pictures we draw?" Lauren asked.

"Yes, very much like that," Catherine said. "Are we ready?"

"Ready," they chorused.

As she drove them to town, she glanced at herself in the mirror to check her hair and noticed she was smiling for no reason. *Oh, my.* Was she excited at the prospect of seeing Collin? *Silly.* She didn't even know him.

As they neared Tucker's Tomes, she was not surprised to see the crowd already gathering there. She moved beyond the center of town and found a parking space within walking distance for the kids. As they hoofed it to the store, she was certain Tucker's Tomes could not accommodate such a crowd.

She was right. The line stretched down the street. As they found the end of the line, an in charge looking woman emerged from Tucker's Tomes with a notepad. She bore an urban sensibility with her black clothes, high heels, smooth coiffed hair, and manicured nails.

She stopped for a moment to speak to those waiting outside. "Hello, everyone. I'm Krysta

Gaines, Collin Donnelly's agent. We're excited for you to be here. I'm getting the names for the inscription in your book to make sure the spelling is correct. Hand the note to Collin when you reach him. Again, thank you for buying *Georgia Birds and Their Stories.*"

The December air had turned a few degrees chillier, and Lauren and John began complaining about being cold. To keep them distracted, Catherine said, "I spy with my little eye, something silver." Right away, the kids started searching for what it might be.

"Is it the doorknob of Gray's Grocery?" Lauren asked.

"Not that," Catherine responded.

"Is it that lady's bracelets?" John asked, pointing to Krysta's arm adorned with several glistening silver and diamond bracelets. She was jotting down the name of the person in front of them.

"Not them, either," Catherine said.

"It's the Christmas bell on the pole," Lauren announced, pointing to a bell on the gas light."

Catherine high fived Lauren. "That's it," she said.

Krysta moved beside them. "How should Collin inscribe your book?" she asked.

"Kids, Mr. Donnelly will write your names in the book, too," Catherine explained.

"Lauren . . ." Lauren said.

"And John," John added.

"Very well," Krysta said in a professional way. She jotted the names down and handed the paper to Catherine. "Thank you for coming." She smiled a million-dollar smile and moved on to a family behind them, her silver bracelets tinkling in her wake.

After about five minutes and another round of I Spy, this time involving something pink that turned out to be the tennis shoes of a girl a few people back, Catherine, Lauren, and John followed the line to the counter where they bought their book from Tucker. Catherine put her purse on the counter, and trying to find her wallet, she pulled a few items from it. Finally, she extracted her debit card from the wallet in her bulging purse. *Why did she always have to carry so much stuff?*

"Good to see you folks in here today," Tucker proclaimed in his usual dramatic voice.

"We're getting Mr. Donnelly's book about birds," John said. "He's going to sign it." John leaned forward. "Kind of like when we sign our drawings."

Tucker laughed. "Thank you—a good explanation, John." He handed Catherine her debit card, her receipt, and gave the children the book.

"Thank you," Lauren and John said in duet fashion.

Tucker nodded. "Thank you."

Then, the kids pivoted and approached Collin. "Hello, Mr. Donnelly," John said. "I liked Otis. He was my favorite."

Collin smiled. "Glad you did, John. He's one of my favorite birds, too, although I think they all may be my favorites."

Krysta reentered the store and walked toward Collin. She leaned over, whispered in his ear, and touched him on the shoulder. He smiled.

It wasn't what she did, but how she did it. Catherine folded her arms across her chest, her eyes narrowing. Was something more here beyond an agent and author relationship? And what was this unexplained clenching in her chest? He signed the book and Catherine mumbled, "Thank you." She couldn't clear out of the store fast enough. She'd promised the kids an ice cream after the book signing so she walked robotically next door to Connie's.

"Hello, to all of you. Have you been to the book signing next door?" Connie asked.

Lauren showed her the book and giggled.

"You've already had fun, and you're about to have more. What kind of ice cream do you want today?"

"Birthday surprise for me, two scoops," John said.

"A daring choice, since it's not even your birthday," Connie said.

Lauren piped, "Christmas Crunch."

"I told your mom to tell you about our new flavor. Glad she did. And Mom?" She paused a moment. "What can I get for you? A wet towel, perhaps. You seem dazed."

"I'm fine. Could I have strawberry. One scoop." She didn't want ice cream, but she hated to be a party pooper.

"One scoop it is." Connie peered at her.

Connie had a sometimes annoying way of seeing what was going on with a person without them telling her. It could be uncomfortable.

Catherine paid for the cones and took the one offered her. They found a table near the front of the store. The crowd from Tuckers still spilled over on the sidewalk, and Krysta moved about smiling, shaking hands, and acting as if she were also Collin's PR woman.

Catherine sighed as she absentmindedly licked her cone. They both loved birds. It seemed a flicker, just a flicker, but now . . . well . . .

Lauren and John's friends, Madison and Ben, emerged from the counter. As they took a seat, John asked, "Mom, can we sit with them?"

Catherine motioned to their mom, and she nodded. Lauren and John streaked over to their table.

29

As they did, Connie slipped into the chair next to Catherine. "Why are you glum?"

Catherine pointed next door. "I'm just being silly."

"Well, I don't know about silly, but what happened with the guy you came in with? When I saw you with him, it was the first time in a long time that I thought you weren't trying not to be sad."

"Maybe, but . . ." She nodded toward the window. "I believe he's already taken. That woman there."

Connie turned around in her seat and studied Krysta a moment, then turned back. "Doesn't seem the type for him."

Connie's radar was not always one hundred percent. "Maybe not, but I think they're an item."

"Be with you in a sec," Connie said to a customer at the counter, then directed her gaze back to Catherine. "Sofia's not here—I'd better go. But you shouldn't close any doors." She rose and went to help the customer, leaving Catherine to ponder her words. She didn't see how she could close a door that was already shut.

She motioned to the kids that she was ready to leave and reached into her purse for her keys. *Where are they?* She pulled out her wallet, her makeup bag, her notepad, her hairbrush, her earbuds, her cell phone. No keys. Then it came to her where they were—*Tucker's.*

Wouldn't you just know it? Maybe she could talk one of the kids into going back for her. Pretty cowardly, getting a kid to do her dirty work. She needed to face the situation. She grabbed the kids' hands, exited Connie's, took a deep breath outside Tucker's Tomes, and reentered. The crowd had dispersed, and Collin was packing to go. She tried to breeze past without him noticing her.

"Catherine, I'm glad you came back. I was about to call you."

Catherine flinched as Tucker called her name.

"I figured these might be yours." Tucker held the keys.

She nodded. "They are. I discovered them missing when we started to leave Connie's. Thank you." She took the keys and ushered the kids back to the door.

"Catherine, I didn't even get a chance to speak with you when you came in before," a voice said as she reached for the doorknob.

Almost a clean getaway. She put her game face on and turned toward Collin. "You know, have to keep moving with kids."

He slipped a notepad into a backpack. "Right. Hey, I was thinking about going to see the old mill tomorrow afternoon. Also, I ran into David Worth, and he heard someone spotted a red-cockaded woodpecker in old growth pine forests beyond the mill. I thought I'd try to take pictures of it, too."

"Aren't those . . ."

"Endangered," Collin said. "Yes, they are. I've never even seen one, except in pictures."

Catherine moved toward the door. "Well, I hope you're successful." She turned the knob.

He moved closer to her. "I was hoping you might go with me."

Catherine looked down at the kids. "No, thank you. We have a lot to do."

Sunday afternoon, the kids were both going to be at a birthday party, but he didn't need to know.

"Hey, Mom, did you forget?" Lauren interrupted. "Esther's birthday party is tomorrow afternoon, and then we're staying for dinner. You can go and see the birds." She smiled in a sweet way.

Collin grinned. "It's settled then." He pointed to the sidewalk. "What do you say? I'll meet you right out there around 2:30—should give us enough time to explore before dusk."

"Sure," Catherine said through a stiff smile. "See you tomorrow." And with that, she scooted the kids outside before anything else could go haywire.

FOUR

On Sunday afternoon, Catherine maneuvered her SUV into a parking spot down from Tucker's Tomes. Collin's white convertible occupied a space a short distance beyond hers. The top was up—a wise choice. The weather had turned cooler, and the temperature would only be a brisk fifty degrees today, more like normal early December weather. She pulled her sweater around her and exited her vehicle, the uncertainty of this adventure causing her muscles to tense.

Collin strode along the sidewalk. "Hey, glad you could make it. Don't you need a coat?"

"I like that it feels more like December," she said, rubbing her arms. "What do you have in mind?"

He gestured toward his car. "Why don't you leave your SUV here and ride with me?"

"I'll grab my purse." She reached in and hefted her bag from the seat, closed the door, and then clicked the lock.

They covered the few steps to his car, and he opened the door for her. It had been forever since she'd sat in a sports car. She lowered herself in as he closed the door, and she snapped her seat belt. It felt like they were preparing for liftoff.

Collin slid into his seat, and a grin eased across his face. "Don't worry, I'm keeping the speedometer in check. Don't want to scare you."

"I appreciate it." As he backed from the space and headed off, she asked, "How did the book signing go?"

"Well, I met a lot of folks."

"Yes, uh . . ." She hesitated as they moved out of downtown Worthville. "I met your agent, Krysta. She seems good at what she does."

Collin paused. "She is. She's helped me a lot."

As Collin's GPS navigated him toward the Worthville Mill, Catherine debated in her head whether to plunge ahead and ask him the question on her mind. What was the point in allowing herself to be attracted to someone who was *already* attached? Just as she determined to speak, Collin did.

"Krysta and I were an item for a while. But for me, our interests seemed incompatible. I appreciate all she's done, but I don't think we could build a life

34

together. I'm not sure she's accepted it, though."
Like that, he'd answered her question.

"You're not dating?"

He shook his head. "No. We haven't for some time."

She let out a breath, and as they hit the county road and space opened in front of them, it seemed a space in her life opened, too. She unconsciously directed her attention to the fence posts and fields whizzing past. Her lips eased into a tiny smile.

A little farther along, Collin flipped his blinker on and turned by the wooden sign that proclaimed, "Worthville Mill, Original Gristmill. Circa 1876." A garland topped the sign, signaling the mill was ready for Christmas.

Collin made the turn onto the winding road.

She nodded as the mill came into view. "Oh, my. It's amazing."

She hadn't seen Genny much in the past month, so she didn't know about all the decorations. "Genny and David must have hired someone to do this. There's no way they could handle it this close to her delivering twins."

"As a matter of fact, they did. David told me they hired a firm specializing in historically appropriate Christmas décor. You know, he's so excited about those new babies coming."

"You knew David and Genny before you came for the signing?"

"David, yes. I've yet to meet Genny. David and I have transacted business online and over the phone. In fact, he's the one who arranged the signing at Tucker's. I met him for the first time when I came to Worthville on this trip."

What business might David and Collin have together? She shifted her attention to the evergreen boughs lining the rails outside the mill and the red-ribboned wreaths that hung from every window. Each one twinkled with light. She imagined the lights a compromise to the historicity, but they amped up the charm.

The giant water wheel turned, water pouring over the paddles, which in turn operated the millstones inside. The freshly ground cornmeal sold at the mill was unparalleled. A pop-up Christmas Tree and Wreath Shop stood a few feet from the parking area, adding to the holiday feeling. Visitors to the Mill strolled around outside, pausing to take in the Mill or check out the trees. For a moment, they, too, studied the various options—spruce, Leyland cypress, and cedar. She might choose a cedar this year, a very old-fashioned choice.

"Shall we?" Collin said, gesturing to the mill.

She headed toward the door. So long since she'd been here. Since before Don died, she guessed.

Collin opened the door for her, and she stepped in. The space buzzed with activity. Children laughing and customers discussing options. The scent of spiced cider floated in the air, instrumental Christmas music played in the background, and Christmas trees decorated in assorted themes lined the wall opposite the wheel mechanism of the mill.

She took a wooden Christmas star in her hand and discovered it handmade. In fact, as she examined other ornaments, they all appeared crafted by hand, too. "Can you believe this?" she asked, holding a wreath of tiny cedar cones with a wee green bow. "Not one of these is imported. They're all regionally made."

Collin surveyed the displays. "Quite an undertaking to source all these in the South. What's this?" He stepped to a tree and plucked a blue bird from it. "This has your name written all over it." He moved to the checkout counter, zapped his debit card, and then returned to her, placing the painted wooden bird in her hand.

She lifted her hand closer to inspect the bird. "Such detail, and the color is vibrant. See the rusty red breast—the same color they are in the wild." She rolled the bird over and peeked to see if a name was inscribed on the bottom. "Wait, this has your name written on it. It says Donnelly Designs. A. Johnson. You're responsible for this?"

Collin laughed. "I didn't paint it, but I designed it. I employ a group of artisans who craft these according to my specifications. Andrea Johnson did this one. Like I said, I want to make people care. The profits from these go to a foundation supporting habitat preservation for endangered species."

Catherine stood there a moment, remembering Genny's question about whether she thought Collin was cute. She studied his brown eyes and the way they crinkled at the edges. "That's interesting," is all she said, and then she remembered her manners. "Thanks for the bird. I love it."

She tucked the ornament into her purse, and they took a few minutes to review the other selections and even a wall of jams and jellies in addition to the Worthville Mill's signature grits and cornmeal products.

"I'll have to come back here when I make my list. There are so many great Christmas gift ideas here," Catherine said.

"Haven't made your list yet?"

"Not yet. For the last couple of years, Christmas has been . . . challenging."

"I imagine it would be." Collin glanced at his smart watch. "Hey, do you mind if we head to the spot David told me about? I'm afraid we're going to lose the light if we don't leave soon. Don't want to miss the RCW's while I'm here."

"RCW's?" she asked, both confused and relieved he changed the subject and didn't ask any more about her grief.

"Just an abbreviation birders use for the Red-cockaded Woodpeckers."

They moved toward the car and stopped to take one more look at the trees.

When they closed the doors, Collin laughed. "I'm not sure we have the right car for this trip. There's a dirt road involved."

"The right car?"

"I also have an SUV in Atlanta. I wish I'd brought it. This car . . . well, Krysta wanted me to buy it. She said she didn't want to ride around looking like she was in an edition of 'Dirt Roads in Georgia.'"

"I see."

She wondered if anyone ever explained to Collin that one shouldn't talk much about an ex-girlfriend, especially on a first date, which she thought this was. If Krysta made him buy a car, their being together wasn't just a few dates. It must have been long term.

David pulled onto Fairview Road from the mill drive and wound back beyond it. "David gave me directions from the mill. No way to use the GPS. He said it wasn't but about four miles. But part of it is on foot."

Sure enough, in what she imagined to be about three miles, Collin turned onto a dirt road that seemed in pretty good condition, so no big bumps, but still they needed to drive slower.

After a few minutes, Collin stopped. "This should be the spot. He said to walk alongside this field and move in from there." He pointed to his right. "Old growth forest lines this field. The RCW is one of the few birds who excavate living trees. It can take them several years to do it." He grabbed his binoculars.

"Several years? Wow, that's commitment to a dwelling," Catherine said as she exited the car and began walking the tree line.

Collin stopped and surveyed the tall pines. "I think we're going to have to go in a ways. What we're looking for is a cavity."

Catherine nodded as they stepped onto the pine needle floor of the forest, the scent of it invigorating. She took in a big breath and scanned the trunks for RCW homes. They hadn't gone in a hundred feet before she spotted a hole about forty feet off the ground.

She stopped Collin and pointed. "Is that what we're looking for?"

His eyes lit up. "It is, and you can tell it's active because of the sap running down the side of the tree. The birds keep the resin wells flowing because it serves as a deterrent to snakes." He handed her the binoculars. "Take a closer look."

She put the binocs to her eyes and studied the woodpecker hole. What an amazing phenomena of nature. After a moment, she intended to give the

40

binoculars back to Collin, but a fluttering bird landed on the tree. She focused the lens—a Red-cockaded Woodpecker—zebra back, white cheek, a tiny red dot under a black cap.

"Oh, my. There it is." She trained her gaze on the bird for a moment and then handed the binoculars to Collin, who also viewed it.

She stood in the forest, looking up, slack jawed. To see this rare bird caused a lightness in her chest and standing in the cathedral of pines made her feel her senses were coming alive again. She'd forgotten all about this big, wide wonderful world because of the daily grind and slugging through the grief process. Reacquainting herself with it was nice. It was kind of like waking.

The last of the sun's golden rays sifted through the branches. Collin looked west. "Looks like we're about to lose the sun. We'd better head back."

On their way to the car, she said, "I haven't been in a forest in ages. Thank you for inviting me." She glanced back once more at the bird's cavity. "Do you think many people know these birds are here?"

"I wouldn't know. I sure hope the landowner does, though, because he'd need to be careful with herbicides, and there are other things to consider as well. You know, the Red-cockaded Woodpecker is a keystone species."

She nodded. "Like bees?"

"Yes. Many other types of wildlife are dependent on them—birds, squirrels, and others use those cavities once they're abandoned."

"God's creation is amazing." She often marveled at the intricacies of it.

They arrived at the car, and he opened the door for her. She got in, and once they fastened their seat belts, he patted her hand. "Thanks for doing this. I don't meet many people who enjoy this kind of thing." His touch on her hand sent ricocheting sensations through her, which made her glad she was already sitting down, since her legs seemed a little weak. If she didn't know better, this felt like the beginnings of a schoolgirl crush.

She shook off the idea. "It was a real treat for me," she said. "I used to go bird watching with my dad. I do a little bit with my kids. When I heard about your bird book, I told Lauren and John about it, and they couldn't wait to get one. I was going to wait until Christmas to give it to them, but meeting you at the book signing was such fun for them." She started to snap her seat belt again, forgetting she'd already done so. Wow was she distracted.

He nodded. "I'm glad." He cranked the car, and as they rolled along in the golden light spilling across the fields, she breathed a sigh edged with excitement.

FIVE

After driving the kids to school on Monday morning, Catherine became aware she was humming under her breath on the way home. What was the tune? She hummed a few notes, and then realized it was the old song about the red robin. She laughed. Her daddy used to sing it to her when she was a little girl. Her mother had died when she was young, and her dad had taken up both roles. His absence in her life was inestimable but sweet memories helped. Well, sometimes they helped. Other times, they just made her cry.

Collin asked her for lunch before he returned to Atlanta today. They were to meet at noon at Della's Deli. She clicked on her blinker and turned into her driveway. As soon as she switched the ignition off, her cell phone rang. She plucked it from her purse. It was Genny.

"Hey, how are you today?" Catherine asked.

43

"I didn't go to work. I can't maneuver well enough. Dr. Fleming's temporary replacement for me was already coming this morning to cover my maternity leave, so I didn't feel too bad about not going in."

Catherine could hear the weariness in her voice. "I'm glad. I think you were pushing yourself too hard. Is there anything you want to do that might be relaxing?"

"Why don't we go for a ride? I need a change of scenery. I can't go to work, but I've been in the house two days. I think I can manage sitting in the car. David is really preoccupied with trying to finish his work."

"I'll be right there." Catherine turned off the phone and put the SUV in reverse.

When she pulled into Genny's yard, she was already standing on the porch and appeared to be wearing David's bowling shirt emblazoned with the words, Worthville Wolves, on the front. Catherine guessed Genny didn't want to invest in huge maternity clothes, so she pilfered items from David's closet. She didn't carry a coat, and the weather was even cooler than yesterday.

Catherine exited the car, covered the distance to the front porch, and took hold of Genny's elbow. Genny waddled to the vehicle, and when Catherine helped her get seated, she asked, "Don't you need a coat? I can fetch one for you."

44

Genny glared at her. "Coat? Are you kidding? I have two portable heaters right here." She patted her stomach. "I'm hot. Where are we going?"

"I don't know. Wherever you want to go."

Catherine went around the car and sat in the driver's seat. Genny stretched the seat belt to its limit, fastened it, then rested her head against the back of the seat. "I just want to go to labor and delivery at the hospital, but it's not time."

The perfect idea came to Catherine. "What about the mill? I bet you haven't even seen the Christmas décor."

"No. I haven't seen anything outside Dr. Fleming's practice and the inside of our home for weeks. David has done the grocery shopping. The mill is a great choice. I would like to see what the Christmas décor company we hired did with the place."

Catherine cranked the car, pulled around in Genny's front yard, and smiled, reflecting on her time at the mill the day before.

"You're smiling," Genny said.

"I smile," Catherine said.

"When you think you're supposed to. You're smiling for real. What is it?"

"Well . . ."

"Spill it. I only talk to people about their illnesses. I need excitement."

"Collin Donnelly and I went to the mill yesterday, and then we went bird watching. We saw an endangered species."

"You mean the reckless tourist, book author, bicycle stealer?"

"That's the one. I found out he supplies bird ornaments for the shop at the mill, and then we went to a nearby forest and found a Red-cockaded Woodpecker."

"Wow. You know, now that I think about it, I believe I do remember David mentioning Collin's name. You looked at Christmas ornaments and birds? Interesting. If it were anyone else but you, I'd think the date a real dud, but I know how much you love birds."

As rolling fields passed, Catherine kept replaying the day before in her mind. Wonderful to have made a new memory.

Genny reached into her purse. "I'm always hungry, so I brought a snack." She extended a cracker pulled from a plastic bag to Catherine. "Want one?"

Catherine eyed the cracker that was smeared with a suspicious green substance.

Genny then dropped a chunk of watermelon on it from another baggy.

"And that is?" Catherine asked.

"Pureed olives with watermelon."

"No, but thanks for offering. I've just had breakfast." Which, if she were honest, she was in danger of losing just looking at the green slime.

Catherine turned in at the Worthville Mill sign and wound down the road. When the wreath bedecked windows came into view, Genny said, "They did a great job. And look at the Christmas tree lot. I love it."

"I do, too. It's coming together."

To Catherine's surprise, Genny was able to navigate the steps to the Mill, and both of them spent a while checking out the decorated Christmas trees. Catherine didn't have time the day before to look at all the birds Collin made, so she examined each species while Genny seemed preoccupied with a children's themed tree.

Catherine took her selections to the checkout counter and as she stood there, Genny sidled up to her. "I take it you like those ornaments." She gestured to the pile of birds Catherine had accumulated at the checkout counter.

Catherine laughed. "I do." She held a bluebird. "I bought this for John's stocking. And this . . ." She lifted a bright yellow goldfinch. "Is for Lauren's."

"But who are the others for?"

"Friends and people who help me during the year, like the lady who does my hair." It was the most progress she'd made on her Christmas list so far. "I hope they like birds as much as I do."

"Thoughtful, but I'm not sure many rival your love for the avian creatures," Genny said. "But even if they don't, the bird ornaments are beautiful."

"You're not getting anything?" Catherine asked as a clerk scanned her items.

"Well, I have an in with the owner. I think he'll give me a discount."

Catherine laughed. "Oh, right. Good deal."

She took her package, and they headed back to the SUV. Genny took her time, seeming a little tired.

Once outside, Catherine turned once more to gaze at the mill. "I do love this place. I'm a little jealous of the employees getting to stay here all the time. The water wheel is so soothing." Then, she turned to Genny and asked, "Do you want to see the woodpecker?"

Genny paused a moment. "Do I have to walk far?"

"Not far."

"Let's do it then."

Catherine turned around and traced the route she and Collin had taken the day before. As dense green forest alternated with rolling fields, a sense of anticipation built in her. She loved the idea of sharing one of nature's secrets with someone else.

When she arrived at the turnoff, she pulled in and moved along the dirt road. She spotted something on the far left side of the field that hadn't been there the day before—a parked SUV. Not only that, a man with what appeared to be a tripod and surveyor's equipment positioned himself facing the forested area she and Collin had explored.

"Oh, no," she said.

"What's going on?" Genny asked.

"I don't know, but why would there be a surveyor here?" Catherine rolled around to where the surveyor stood.

"Hi, we came to see the Red-cockaded Woodpeckers on this land. Is someone selling it?"

The surveyor scratched something on a pad and looked up. "Yep."

"Any idea who might buy it?"

"Nope." The surveyor adjusted his tripod.

She was getting nowhere with this monosyllabic man. "Can we see if the birds are there? We don't want to be arrested for trespassing."

The man shrugged. "Makes no difference to me."

Finally, a sentence. They wouldn't be long, so she pulled over. Catherine opened the console and rummaged around. She pulled a pair of yellow toy binoculars from it. "I thought these were in here. They're not high-powered ones, but they're pretty good. I think we'll be able to see the bird at least."

She and Genny exited, took a few steps into the forest, and then Catherine turned to her. "You're going to love this. It's exciting to see a rare bird."

"I'm sure I will." Genny took a step, and a stick cracked under the pressure.

Catherine's gaze slid to the source of the noise, and an alarm went off in her. "Your ankles. They're swollen."

Genny glanced to her feet. "Oh, my. I need to elevate my feet. I hadn't noticed I was retaining fluid."

They weren't more than thirty feet from where she'd parked. Catherine whisked, or as much as she could whisk a woman pregnant with twins back to the vehicle, and they took off.

Pangs of regret rose in her. What was she thinking, dragging a woman this close to delivery way out here? It must have been one of the worst decisions she'd made lately.

In a few minutes, they rolled into Genny's yard. Catherine helped her into the house, and then positioned an ottoman against the sofa so Genny could put her feet on it. "I am sorry, Genny. I couldn't live with myself if something happened to you or the babies."

"Taking a ride was my idea. Going to the mill sounded like a great adventure for someone who's been housebound. I'm the one with the poor judgment."

"What can I get you?"

Genny stuffed a pillow behind her. "Some water . . ." She paused. "And maybe artichoke hearts with a strawberry toaster pastry."

The combination revolted Catherine, but she said, "No problem."

"Thanks. I'll eat, and then I think I'm going to take a nap."

"Right away." Catherine moved to the kitchen and stood at the sink, filling a glass with tap water. When Genny first moved back here, she fought against an unscrupulous land developer who tried to seize her property and destroy her home.

The glass brimmed with cool water, and she turned off the tap. Could a sinister development plot be unfolding and threatening the RCW land? Could someone like that terrible Saul Lance who'd gone after Genny's home be putting the woodpeckers in danger of destruction? Laws were in place to prevent such a thing.

Genny already had as much as she could deal with. Catherine opted not to say anything else to her. She spotted the toaster pastry box on the counter, opened the refrigerator to find a jar of artichoke hearts already opened, and placed a few on a plate along with the pastry. *Yuck.*

When she carried the water and food back to the living room, Genny was dozing. Catherine put it all on a table and slipped out, locking the door behind her.

She cranked the SUV and was thankful for the lunch date with Collin. He would know what to do.

After covering the few miles into town, when she arrived at Della's Deli, the place was almost empty. She checked her watch—11:45.

Della waved at her. "Take your pick of tables. The calm before the storm."

Catherine laughed as she chose one near the front window. She put her purse on a chair and scanned the menu board, although she knew what she wanted. Nothing beat Della's egg salad. With that decided, she turned her attention to the goings on outside the window.

Alexander from the hardware store zipped past on foot, appearing to be on a mission. Probably to the bank or post office. Tim Bouvier ambled by with a cup from Your Yogurt, appearing delighted with his choice judging from the smile on his face.

Across the street, David's convertible pulled into a space right in front of Tucker's Tomes. She smiled at the BRDSRUS tag and how infuriated she'd been the first time she saw it. Then, right beside his car, another car pulled in.

Krysta emerged and strolled up to Collin, slipped her arm around his, and together, they went into Tucker's Tomes. Krysta? She assumed Krysta had already headed back to Atlanta. And there she sat, waiting for him. For the second time that morning, she had to ask, *what am I thinking?*

Catherine's shoulders slumped, and she swallowed hard. She felt as if she were a big bubble and someone was letting the air out of her. Deflated, that's the word she'd used.

The reality was Krysta was a fixture in David's life. Catherine didn't even know if David understood the power of that. After what she'd been through, the last thing she wanted to do was compete for someone's attention. She grabbed her purse from the table and headed for the door.

"Leaving so soon," Della called after her.

"I just remembered something," she said, which was the absolute truth. As she closed the door, she remembered she still wasn't ready. She didn't think she'd ever be ready for this.

SIX

A little after noon, her cell phone rang. The number wasn't familiar to her, but she could guess who it was. She clicked it off, stepped outside, and took a seat in a chair with a view of the birdfeeder. She tried to shake off the situation with Collin, and instead, focused on what she could do about the potential threat to the woodpeckers.

A black and white chickadee popped onto the bird feeder dowel and eyed her.

"I know. I know," she said. "I'm trying to think of something."

She typed "Fairview Road, for sale" into a search on her phone. The first three results didn't match, but the fourth was for sure the place she and Collin visited. Under the sale price, in small letters, read, "Sale pending."

Hmm, an offer was already on the table. *Oh, my.* Was this one of those deals people work out between themselves before the property ever goes on the market. But which people?

She took a deep breath. Maybe she was jumping to conclusions. No reason to believe anything sinister was happening. Wouldn't she have heard if someone were going to do something drastic?

Then again, her circle was pretty small.

Her phone rang again, and Genny's name flashed on the screen. She pressed the green button..

"Catherine, something's wrong. Can you take me to the hospital?"

Her adrenaline kicked in, causing her heart to race. "I'll be right there."

Catherine grabbed her keys and purse, bolted to the door, and in less than a minute, she pulled into Genny's driveway across the road.

She flew to the door, but Genny was already coming through it, grimacing in pain. Catherine didn't ask questions.

"Take my arm," she said and helped Genny into the vehicle while, all the time, Elizabeth the hen squawked and flapped about as if a fox were in the yard. Somehow, she must have sensed the trouble.

As they zipped to the hospital, she was more convinced than ever that they did too much that morning. This was six weeks before her due date.

55

Genny needed to hang on a little while longer for the sake of the babies.

"I've already called David." Genny winced. "He's meeting us there. It was faster to have you take me rather than wait for him to come home." She patted the pocket in her sweater. "Oh, no, I left my cell phone."

"Don't worry, I have mine, and David has his. You won't need it." *Oh, Lord, please let Genny and the babies be okay*, she prayed under her breath. She tried to keep her speed under control, but her foot weighed heavy on the pedal, pushing them past the speed limit.

At the hospital, she pulled right in front of the emergency entrance, dashed inside, and to a woman sitting behind a desk with a Christmas tree on it, she proclaimed, "Dr. Genny Sanders-Worth, seven and one-half months pregnant with twins. In pain."

The woman jumped up, grabbed a wheelchair, and hurried to the SUV with Catherine.

"Dr. Worth, don't you worry," she said as she assisted Genny into the chair. "You've always taken good care of your patients, and we're going to take good care of you."

"Her husband is on the way," Catherine said.

They rolled into the hospital and toward a set of double doors.

"You stay here, and when he comes, have him press this button here and identify himself"—the woman pointed to a buzzer beside the doors—"and we'll get him back to see her."

Catherine nodded as the woman disappeared with Genny.

David sprinted into the waiting room, out of breath. "How is she?" he panted.

"I don't know. She was in pain. They've taken her back." She pointed to the button. "You press that and identify yourself."

David did so, and the doors swung open. Catherine planted herself in a chair as he disappeared down a hallway. She checked her watch. Two hours until she retrieved the kids from school. Hunger pangs rumbled in her stomach. She never ate lunch, so maybe she'd hunt down a vending machine. She was a nervous eater, anyway.

She inquired of another woman seated behind a desk about the vending machines, and then snaked her way around the hallways to an alcove where a line of machines stood. Overwhelmed by the choices, after a few minutes, she settled on a package of cheese crackers.

As she munched on the crackers on the way back to the waiting room, a twinge of regret about ditching the lunch with David came over her. She would like to have talked to him about the RCW dilemma. She rounded a corner into a waiting room where David stood, glancing around.

"I'm here," she said.

He turned in her direction. "Oh, good. I thought I'd come and tell you we're going to be a while. She'll definitely have to stay the night. Maybe longer. They're going to do a few more tests, but after a preliminary exam, the doc thinks they can control this, and then Genny will have to be on bed rest for the duration of the pregnancy."

"Oh, my. That's a challenge."

"It is, especially with no family in the area."

"But, we can do this. I'll call around and see who is available, and we'll have folks with her anytime you're at work."

"Thank you for doing this. I'll have to cut back my schedule, but I have work I must finish before the baby comes. I can do some from home." David rubbed his furrowed brow, his concern obvious.

"Don't worry. It's going to be fine." Catherine slipped the cracker package into her purse.

"No need for you to stay. I'll let you know the timeline once we know more."

Catherine gave David a hug and turned to go.

"And Catherine," David said.

She turned back.

"Genny told me to tell you your outing this morning had nothing to do with her situation. Stop feeling guilty."

Catherine nodded. "Thanks." Then she headed to the parking lot. Just like Genny to think of others when she was in pain.

She reached her vehicle, and as she backed from the parking space, she was already making a list in her mind of people who could stay with Genny, even for a half day. Genny's coworkers were a no-go, because they would be working similar hours to David.

There was Connie, who seemed to be taking more days off since she'd made Sofia the assistant manager, and Louvene, David's secretary, who could have more availability as David was working from home.

Earlene Bouvier was also a possibility. Earlene might also know retired women in her Bible study who had time to spare. And, of course, herself. This would work.

When she pulled into her driveway, a bluebird shot across her path toward a box hanging on a tree. Seeing the bird reminded her of the dilemma near the mill.

What would she do?

She moved the gearshift to park and against her better judgment, she called the unknown number that had appeared on her cell phone earlier.

"Hello," a familiar voice said.

"Collin?" she asked.

A moment passed, and he said, "Catherine, what happened? As soon as I walked into the deli, Della told me you'd left."

"I'm sorry," she said. "Something came up."

"I'm sorry I missed you," he said. "I was a little late getting there. Krysta was on her way to work with another client, and she stopped by to work out a date with Tucker for that author. I needed to go in and pick up extra books I'd brought along for the signing. It took a little longer than I thought because we wound up discussing my next signing."

"Collin, you don't owe me an explanation. I just met you. We're friends. Nothing more."

A pause. "Sure. Friends."

"But I do need your help." She relayed what she'd seen earlier and how she'd found the property listed online with a pending sale.

"Oh, wow. It could be that the people involved in the sale don't know about those birds. I was going to go back to Atlanta today, but I need to take more pictures of them." He paused. "Do you want to come with me?"

Before she knew what she was saying, "Sure," popped out of her mouth. She checked her watch. "But I need to pick up the kids in a few minutes."

"Bring them along. I'd love to show them the woodpeckers, too."

Lauren and John would be excited to see Collin again, and seeing the birds would be a treat for them.

"Okay, would 3:30 work for you?" she asked.

"Sounds perfect. Meet in front of Tuckers?"

"Sounds great."

Catherine clicked off the phone and sat there a moment. This day had been a roller coaster. First, with Genny, and now with Collin. She'd skipped their lunch, and now she was going off with him again . . . with her kids in tow. What was the word to describe the way she felt? Flustered. Right, her dad used to describe himself that way whenever life seemed erratic.

What was with her where Collin was concerned? It was yes, no, yes, no. She couldn't remember a time she was this wishy-washy. But, since she'd already said yes, on their way back, they could stop by the mill and buy a Christmas tree and wreath for her front door. Her house was lacking any sign of the upcoming holiday. She'd been waiting on a time they all could go together. Might as well make the most of her flakey decision.

SEVEN

As Catherine and her kids sat in front of Tucker's Tomes, Collin parked, and she waved for him to get in the SUV. No way they'd all fit in his convertible.

He opened the passenger door, slid in, and turned to Lauren and John. "Good to see we have a couple of expert bird spotters with us. Are you excited about seeing the woodpeckers?"

Lauren and John let go simultaneous hoots of joy. "They're en-dan-nerd," John tried to say.

"They are, so it's extra special to see one." He turned to Catherine. "You okay? You seem a little stressed."

His emotional radar must come from being an observant writer. "I'm fine. Genny went into labor today, and I had to take her to the hospital. They thought they could stop the contractions, but she'll be on bed rest."

"Is Dr. Genny okay?" Lauren asked in a worried tone.

She should have already told the kids., but she had so much racing through her mind. "She's fine. The babies tried to come a little early, but they're going to wait a little longer now."

"I can't wait for those babies to get here," Lauren said. "When I'm old enough, I'm going to babysit them." Having twin babies across the street was a dream come true for Lauren. She received twin dolls one Christmas when she was younger that she lugged around until their heads were bald. Catherine thought Lauren believed the real babies coming this year at Christmas were a special gift for her.

Catherine shifted her thoughts back to the woodpeckers. "You're taking pictures of the birds. And then what happens?"

"I'm going to send the pictures to the state Fish and Wildlife Service. They'll need to investigate. But sometimes, it takes them a while."

"We can't bother David about this, but in the meantime, I bet David's secretary, Louvene, could shed light on who the buyer is. She knows everything. And if she doesn't, she can find out."

Collin laughed. "I've talked with her before. She is an in-charge kind of woman."

"In fact, I have to call her about staying with Genny, I could ask her about it then."

"Sounds good," Collin said.

They passed the mill and turned to the right. When they arrived at the property, there was no sign of activity, but a few poles with flags dotted the landscape, evidence of the surveyor's work.

Catherine pulled alongside the road where they'd parked the other day. She helped the kids out, and they strode through the forest hand in hand, a kid on each side of her, following Collin.

"Wow," John said. "This is neat. It's like the trees are making a tent around us."

"It is," Catherine said.

Collin pointed. "There's one of the cavities."

Catherine gestured to it. "Look, Lauren and John. That's where the Red-cockaded Woodpeckers live—the hole with the sap running down."

Wings flashed, and a bird lit on the tree. "Is that it?" John said a little too loudly.

Catherine put her finger to her lips. "That's it," she said. "Let's watch."

Collin maneuvered around, snapping pictures. The bird positioned himself to keep them in view, then disappeared into the hole.

"I wonder if this tree is part of a grouping." Collin edged closer for a better shot.

"Grouping?" Catherine asked.

"The birds tend to nest in groups. They're very sociable. I like that about them."

She turned to him. "I like that about them, too."

64

He smiled, and then they followed the forest path, and sure enough, on either side of it, a dozen trees showed the obvious marks of RCW habitation.

"I've never seen anything like it." Catherine wished her father could have witnessed this. It would have thrilled him like it did her.

Collin didn't speak but clicked away, trying to capture the extent of the bird's presence. Oh, what a tragedy for someone to come in and destroy this forest. If she had the money, she would buy it to preserve this sanctuary for the birds. An occasional bird would flit about, which elicited a gasp from Lauren or John.

The birds and their cavities grew harder to see as the light lessened in the forest. Collin turned to Catherine. "We'd better go. I don't want to be here with the kids trying to find our way back in the dark."

"I'm not afraid," John declared.

Collin stooped over to make eye contact with John. "I'm sure you're not, but unless we have eyes like cats, it would be hard to see in the dark."

John nodded seemingly satisfied he would not be accused of being a baby in these circumstances.

On the way back to the vehicle, Catherine said, "Collin, do you mind stopping by the mill for a few minutes? We still haven't purchased a Christmas tree, and I thought while we were in the vicinity . . ."

"You bet," he said.

"Yay!" squealed the kids.

When they'd piled into her SUV, Collin reached over and clicked on the radio. "Let's have a little Christmas music to get us ready for the tree purchase."

They jingle belled together all the way to the mill. When they arrived and parked, the kids barreled straight for the Christmas tree lot. It didn't hurt that they were serving free, hot apple cider.

After they'd all been served, and they were meandering around looking at trees, Collin asked, "What kind of tree did you have in mind?"

Catherine pointed to a wispy one. "I was thinking cedar, but you never know what the kids might think, and I kind of leave it to them." And then a thought dropped into her brain. "I hope we're not taking too long. You're probably ready to head back to Atlanta. I should have asked you earlier."

Collin held out a hand. "No problem. I called Betty and booked another night. She was quite accommodating. Said I could stay as long as I wanted, till the week before Christmas."

Catherine nodded as the kids stepped to a tall cedar "This is it, Mom," Lauren called.

"Look how huge it is," John said.

It was big, but her ten-foot ceilings should accommodate it. How amazing they should choose that one.

"I think we have a winner," she said to one of the teenage lot attendants with a name tag that read *Sam*. "Could you cut a couple of branches off the bottom, so it fits into the stand?"

"Will do," Sam said, sounding up to the task.

Collin and Sam put the tree on the top of her SUV and tied it to the rack. She also grabbed a couple of fresh wreaths, one for the front door and one for the back. She loved the smell of evergreens as she entered the house.

On the way back to town, John said, "Mr. Collin, are you going to help decorate our tree? I mean, we could use someone tall to hang the ornaments at the top."

"Yeah," Lauren said. "You're the perfect size. And you could eat dinner with us, too."

Catherine let go a nervous laugh. "I'm sure Mr. Collin has better things to do tonight." Although, she agreed he was the perfect size as she took in his tall frame.

Collin turned to her. "I don't. I'd love to join you."

"It's going to be potluck, leftover vegetable soup. And maybe some cornbread I'll throw together."

"Sounds perfect."

Oh, wow. She hadn't seen this coming. She thought about the disarray in the house she hadn't straightened, since she'd been going all day. Oh, well. There was nothing to do about it.

They turned into the driveway, and she ran in to retrieve a pair of cutters for Collin to clip the tree off the roof. Then she brought him the tree stand. Sam did a good job of getting the tree trimmed, so it slipped right into the stand, and then they brought it into the house where it proceeded to overwhelm her den.

"Wow," she said as the branches relaxed into the space. "I was excited about it being cedar and didn't realize how big around it was. I think we're going to have to move the sofa."

Collin helped her maneuver it around to give the tree a little more room. Then he grinned as he stood back to take in the tree. "Hope you have a lot of ornaments."

"Tons," John said with authority. "Lauren and I have our own boxes, too."

"Can't wait to see those," Collin said as he squatted to give the screws around the tree stand a final check.

"I'll fetch water for the tree. Do you mind getting the decorations from the hall closet? We don't have a themed tree—only a bunch of stuff we've collected over the years. I'll warm the soup. And what about a grilled cheese to go with it?"

"I love grilled cheese," Lauren said. "It's one of my favorite foods."

Collin patted her on the back. "We have that in common."

She stood there for a moment and watched the three of them go down the hall. Then, Lauren and John opened the closet door and gave Collin instructions. He began fetching boxes from the closet and bringing them to the den.

She turned and went into the kitchen to start dinner . . . and retrieve a pitcher of water for the tree. She'd need to put "water tree" on the refrigerator or they'd be left with big brown sticks in their house.

The corners of her mouth turned up. She was smiling. Not because she needed to, not because she had to, not because she wanted to make someone think she was okay. She smiled because of a surprising rising contentment.

Even though the meal was thrown together, Collin seemed to enjoy it. After they'd eaten their soup, decorated the tree, and Collin lifted John so he could put the star on the top, they stood back to take it all in. Lauren and John's ornaments, mostly animated characters, sports figures, and princesses were near the bottom because they insisted on placing them themselves. More expensive ornaments of crystal or glass and ornaments from their travels were placed near the top.

69

"I know you said you didn't have a theme, but . . ." Collin held one of the many crystal and glass birds she'd accumulated.

"Yeah, I guess it wasn't intentional, but it does look like the Eastern Flyway for bird ornaments. It just kind of happened."

It's true that she spurned themed trees in favor of a more sentimental family one, but the birds kind of took over. The birds and the red ribbon looping around the tree did tie everything together, though.

Collin followed the extension cord to the outlet. "Is everyone ready?"

"Ready," they chorused as he inserted the plug, and the lights blazed to the ceiling on the enormous tree. Breathtaking.

Lauren hugged her mother. "It's the most beautiful tree I've ever seen. It's like a fairytale tree."

Collin turned to her. "I think it's the most beautiful tree I've ever seen, too."

"Me, too," John echoed, starry eyed.

Collin slipped his hand around her shoulders, and her heart did a little dance. She wanted to freeze frame the moment in her mind. Who would have guessed this circumstance earlier today?

Later, they loaded in the SUV to take David back to his car in town. "Thanks for this," he said as they pulled into town, the flickering of the gas lights lending a charm she'd forgotten about as she didn't often venture downtown at night that much.

"Bring back memories of your childhood?" Catherine asked.

"I was an only child, and each of my parents were also the only child to their parents so our Christmases were small. But we still had fun. I missed having siblings and a bigger family, though."

"I can understand that. Thank you for introducing me to the birds and being such a sport about tonight."

"It was my pleasure," he said as they parked. He turned to the kids. "And thanks for the best Christmas tree decorating party ever."

"You're welcome," John replied. "You did a good job."

"You were a big help," Lauren added.

David gave her a wave. "See you soon," he said., "And let me know how Genny is. Oh, and I'll be in touch about the RCW's. I'll contact the Fish and Wildlife Service, first thing."

"Will do," she said.

He exited and strode to his car. She shifted the gears to reverse, backed out, and headed toward home. She didn't know David. Not much about his family or his past. But she did know he was great with kids, he loved birds, and was willing to take on her leftover vegetable soup.

She told herself again that they were just friends, as she had declared earlier. But somehow, she wondered if her declaration was unraveling a little.

EIGHT

The next morning, she awoke, swung her legs over the side of the bed and reflected a moment on the circuitous route of the day before, which was wholly unanticipated. Who would have guessed the man she'd run out of Della's to avoid meeting would be the same man who'd share such a special time with her family. She rose to go to the bathroom, and when she returned, the phone on the bedside table rang and flashed Genny's number, which meant David must have brought Genny's phone to the hospital.

"Genny, how are you?" she answered.

"Much better, thanks. They've gotten everything under control, and they say they're going to discharge me today."

"I'm glad. I'm calling around this morning to see who might be able to stay with you while David works."

73

"Thanks, but David said we won't need anyone until Thursday, because he can work at home until then. And I'll be fine alone."

Catherine shook her head. "Dr. Sanders-Worth, are you kidding me? There's no way we're leaving a bed-confined woman who's almost eight months pregnant alone."

Genny laughed. "Have it your way, then. I appreciate it."

"How's the food there?"

"I'm missing all my usual snacks. Really tasteless stuff here like graham crackers and yogurt. I can't wait to get home and have prunes in tomato juice. Yum."

Catherine cringed, her taste buds shrinking in fear. "Alright, then. See you later."

They hung up. As Catherine pulled on her clothes, in her head, she clicked through the list she'd made. She'd start with Louvene.

After she'd taken the kids to school, she sat at the kitchen table with coffee and pressed the contact info for David's office. It would be good to speak to Louvene again. She'd gotten to know her when David handled the matters with Don's estate.

On her first try, she heard, "David Sanders, Attorney at Law, Louvene speaking."

"Hi, Louvene. This is Catherine. I hope you're doing okay."

"I am, but ready for those babies. I can't wait."

"You and Lauren, both. I think she's almost as excited as Genny and David. I'm sure you know about Genny's situation, and I'm trying to arrange a schedule for friends to stay with her until she delivers the babies."

"Well, you can put me down for Saturday morning—my usual day off. I know David has a couple of appointments outside the office that morning. He's trying to squeeze in as much as possible before the babies come. I've told him and told him he needed to ease up. Why he doesn't listen is beyond me."

Catherine cleared her throat. It was always hard to tell whether David was Louvene's boss or Louvene was David's. She often acted as if she were the superior, having been assistant to David's predecessor for many years.

"Thank you. That will be a big help. Saturday it is. And Louvene . . .?"

"Yes?"

"I wondered if you wouldn't mind poking around to see if you can find who bought a piece of property over on the Fairview Road. It's a personal matter."

"Well, I don't mind a bit. Can't check anything online, because Worthville is still in the stone age.

But I'm going over to the courthouse in a little while, anyway. What's this about the personal concern?"

She didn't want to let anyone know she was nosing around if there was nothing to be concerned about. "No big deal. I just wondered who bought it."

"I'll check right into it," Louvene said. "Text me the address and count on seeing me Saturday."

She refilled her coffee cup and pressed on with the next call to Connie.

When she answered, Catherine said, "Hey, Connie . . ."

"Catherine, have you spoken with Genny this morning?" she interrupted. "I've been concerned. One of the nurses at Dr. Flemings was in yesterday afternoon and told me what happened. I couldn't get her or David to answer their cell phones yesterday."

"I think she may have left it at home, but she has it now. We were in such a hurry to reach the hospital, we walked out without it. David probably turned his off. But she's okay. Doctors have gotten things calmed, but she needs to be on bed rest, so I'm arranging for folks to stay with her."

"I'm in. I'll take Friday all day—my day off. Sofia has everything under control here, and we have no catering on Friday. Next week is a different story, though. The Christmas parties ramp up."

"We're glad for Friday. I thought I'd call Earlene Bouvier and see if a few women in her Bible study can help, since Genny and David have been going to the study at their house."

Earlene had also babysat John and Lauren a good bit, so Catherine knew she was reliable.

"That's a great idea. Michael and I have enjoyed the study. Great people there."

Catherine jotted Connie's name on Friday. If Catherine did Thursday, this week was covered. Next week was another case, since she'd committed to a couple of volunteer things at the kid's school, with it being the last days before Christmas break, but she anticipated Earlene would be able to help. Some school systems released kids only a couple of days before Christmas. Worthville kids got out a few days earlier than that, which was similar to what Catherine experienced when she was a child. However, it did compress the time she had to prepare for Christmas.

When she reached Earlene she was sitting shotgun while she and Tim delivered care packages to shut ins. After telling her about Genny's situation, she said, "Don't you worry about a thing. I'll make a few calls, and we'll have the calendar covered in no time. Our folks would be glad to help get those babies here safely."

She thanked Earlene and hung up. She and Tim were two of the most giving people in Worthville.

Movement caught her eye in their backyard near a little water feature pond, which Don installed before he became sick. The pond boasted a small waterfall, and the few lily pads they'd put in at first had multiplied. After Don died, she'd spent many hours by it listening to the soothing tumbling water. From behind an azalea bush, a crane with a red crown emerged, a magnificent bird. Likely on the way south from northern breeding grounds. She studied it a moment and decided it was probably a sandhill crane.

She reached over to the dog-eared bird identification book lying with other volumes on the table. She flipped to the page referenced for sandhill cranes and found she was right. The picture matched exactly.

When she put the book back on the table, the cover fell open. "Steve Wood," read the name inscribed on the fly leaf. Her dad. He would have loved to see this bird, too. And the RCW. And the grandchildren with the Christmas tree. Though she would have wanted to share these bird discoveries with her dad, it also made her feel as if she were continuing something he gave her. Something of him was going forward in her kids, too, because they shared this interest.

She studied the bird and remembered reading about wilderness therapy for returning vets—how the awe and wonder of God's creation helped them deal with PTSD. The bird cocked its head as if eyeing her. Maybe the beauty of nature helped one deal with grief as well. The crane flapped its wings, preparing for liftoff, and then took to the skies, its long legs protruding behind it.

"Goodbye," she said. "Thanks for dropping by." The bird seemed yet another gift in a time of unanticipated happenings. She found herself wanting to tell Collin about it.

From the stack on the table, she pulled a volume of devotions she'd read through the years and turned to the one for December 8th. Interesting. The scripture was Ecclesiastes 3:1, the same verse Connie had posted on her wall.

The author was writing about the fall and how her changing leaves lasted a little longer that year. Then, she went on to relate the changes to the seasons in our lives. Catherine read, "Changing seasons in our lives can be a challenge—often a difficult challenge." *True.* "Just as the leaves in my yard have held on this year, I've found myself at times clinging to the season I'm in rather than embrace a new era in my life."

Catherine paused a moment and remembered the words Genny spoke to her about keeping her options open. Was she keeping her options open? She didn't want to cling to this season of grief because she was too afraid of what changes might do to their lives.

She read on. "The changeless One calls us forward and promises to hold us fast through every transition."

Hold us fast. That's what she wanted—to be held and not feel as if she were swinging in space.

She closed the book. After those two losses, it was as if her life reset. Waking early in the morning. Not being able to go back to sleep. Plastering a smile on her face for the sake of the kids. She'd have a good day or a few good hours, and then the grief would sneak in from nowhere and whack her.

"To everything there is a season . . ." she said aloud.

Something in her rose to those words. And yet, at the same time, her heart rate quickened like it did when anxiety crept in.

She glanced at her watch. She needed to head into town to Gray's Grocery. She wanted to buy the candy for stocking stuffers before Mr. Gray sold out. She made the mistake of waiting too late last year and got stuck with dark chocolate bars, green lollipops, and licorice sticks. Her poor children gave her the most pitiful looks when they opened their stockings on Christmas morning. Though they didn't complain . . . she knew.

The thing that saved the day was she'd also found the most amazing kaleidoscopes last minute at Harry's Hardware. "Only reason I have any of those left," Alexander had said, giving his Harry's

Hardware cap a twist, "is because the shipment came late."

She was grateful he was a kid at heart and loaded into the toys at Christmas. She needed to get moving on her Christmas shopping while the kids were going to school. Eight more school days, and they'd be at home all the time. Then it would be next to impossible unless she ordered online. Plus, she wanted to prepare food for Genny so she could take it when she went on Thursday, and she needed supplies.

She grabbed her purse from the table and headed for Gray's Groceries.

As she stood before the Christmas candy display there, she was surprised to see so many different offerings. She placed a couple of chocolate reindeer in her basket. Then she chose two rainbow colored lollipops—should make up for the green ones. Next, she selected bags of bright bubble gum, usually a no-no, but she made an exception at Christmas. When she reached for a gingerbread house kit, another hand came from nowhere and grabbed the same one.

"Oh, I'm sorry," she said. "I'll choose another one."

"No, I want them all," a familiar voice said and laughed.

She spun around. "Collin, I can't believe it. I thought you'd be on your way back to Atlanta."

81

"Funniest thing. When I reached Betty's Bed and Breakfast last night, she said she'd make me a super deal if I wanted to stay until the 20th, since she didn't have anyone else coming in till then. It seemed like an offer I couldn't refuse. I can work from anywhere. I have all my painting supplies and plenty of reference photos to work from, so I'm set. Plus, I'd like to stick around to do more photography. Worthville has a lot to offer. Wish I had my other car." He pointed toward the street. "The convertible out there is a wash for any off-road adventures."

"Well," she said. "You could use my SUV, if you wanted. It's old, but reliable."

"Hmmm. I might take you up on that offer."

"I saw a sandhill crane in my backyard this morning. Wish you could have gotten a shot of him."

"A sandhill? Wow, what a treat to see one in this area. I'm jealous."

She knew he would be. She lifted a gingerbread house kit. "Did you really want all of them?"

He laughed again. "No, one will do, thank you. For my niece and nephew. I think they can share. See you around?"

"See you around," she said. Interesting turn of events. In her heart, a tiny twinge of hope had her wishing his change of plans had something to do with her.

NINE

L oaded with a chicken casserole, the Southern staple for any event in which someone needed to be comforted, French bread, and a lemon pie for dessert, Catherine made her appearance at Genny's on Thursday. She'd spent most of the day before cooking. She may have gone a little overboard on the quantity.

As David met her at the car and she loaded his hands with the food, he said, "Wow, I'm going to have to make room in the refrigerator."

"Oh, and I also brought chicken salad and fruit for lunch." She reached into the backseat for a thermal bag.

As they went inside, unable to keep the screen door from slamming behind them with their hands so full, Genny called from the sofa, "Is that all for me? You know I have to keep up my strength with all the work I'm doing."

"Very funny," Catherine said. "No, it's not all for you. But I do sometimes lose my perspective when cooking. You may have to freeze some of this."

The Christmas tree appeared to be in the same half-decorated shape it was in when she visited the week before. She knew what she'd be doing all day.

"No prob," David said. "We're going to need food when the twins arrive. Would you like coffee?"

"Sure," she said, following him into the kitchen. In her rush, she'd skipped coffee this morning.

David maneuvered items around in the refrigerator and slid the casserole in, then took the other items and found a place for them. He reached for a mug emblazoned with "Worthville Family Practice" and poured dark brew from a coffee pot. He held a pitcher. "Cream?"

"Yes, please." She added the cream, stepped back into the living room with Genny, and took a seat.

"I don't have to leave for work for a few minutes, so could I join you, too."

"Please do, sweetie," Genny said, lifting her head from the pillow. She shuffled her feet around on the sofa and tried to get comfortable. The pained expression on her face said she wasn't successful. David slid into a side chair.

"I hear you and Collin have been seeing each other?" David asked.

The unexpected question caused Catherine to splash coffee on the table when she put her cup down. She reached for a nearby napkin to mop it up. "I wouldn't say we are seeing each other. No, we're friends."

David studied her a moment. "Friends?"

Catherine nodded.

"Hmm. Well, if you say so."

"David . . ." Genny said. "What are you getting at?"

"I think Collin may see things differently. You know, he's a nice guy. I've gotten to know him since we've been buying products from him at the mill. Diagnosed with cancer a few years back but fought his way through it. Amazing to see how he's doing now."

"Cancer?" Catherine blinked, her shoulders growing tight.

"Yeah, melanoma. Had to have several surgeries and radiation."

"I didn't know." She dropped her head. *Melanoma?* The same disease that took Don. She shook off thoughts of his last days.

"Catherine, are you okay?" Genny tried to sit, her expression full of concern.

"I'm fine. Please don't sit up. We don't need to make any more premature trips to the hospital."

David stood and smoothed the creases in his pants. "I guess I'd better go. Louvene will be calling to see where I am. Sometimes, I wonder why I even go in. She can pretty much do everything I do."

They laughed at the truth of it. David kissed Genny goodbye, disappeared, being careful not to slam the screen door, and then his car rolled from the yard.

"I'm going to make myself useful by decorating this tree." Catherine rose to face the job.

"Sorry. It kept falling to the bottom of the list with everything else going on."

"I understand, but you need a cheerful environment."

Catherine started by rearranging the lights that appeared to have been thrown on the tree. She took the time to secure them, then proceeded to wind colorful plaid ribbon around the tree. "I love this ribbon," she said.

"My grandmother used the plaid ribbon on the tree. I love it, too, and it kind of goes with a farmhouse aesthetic. Not that I've been that concerned with any kind of aesthetic in recent times." Genny patted her stomach. "Hey, you grew quiet when David mentioned Collin and his cancer."

Catherine nodded as she took bright red satin balls and placed them on the tree. She scanned the ornament collection. Not many glass—lots of cloth angels, stars, and animals of various kinds, probably made by her grandmother Agnes. Good they were fabric. In a short time, those twins would be rampaging the Christmas tree.

"I didn't mean to. It hit me that he faced the same thing Don did, but Don lost his battle." She would have dodged this question if she could. It was hard to talk about. The melanoma was aggressive and had already spread when found. Doctors couldn't do much. Catherine grimaced at the thought.

She opened another box of ornaments and couldn't believe what it contained. "Oh, my," she said.

"You must have opened the box of painted ornaments. As you can see, Grandmother made cloth birds, then painted them to look like cardinals, bluebirds, chickadees, and the list goes on."

"But this one? How did she know about this one?" Catherine held a beautiful example of a Red-cockaded Woodpecker.

Genny lifted a magazine from a table. "I have no idea, but she didn't like to paint from someone else's picture. She liked to take her own photos and go from there."

Did Agnes know about the RCWs? Amazing. She hung the bird high in the tree. "This is the endangered bird I was going to show you in the

87

woods near the Worthville Mill. Did you know David is the one who told Collin about it?"

"He didn't mention it to me, but then we've been operating on a need to know basis for some time. So when David mentioned Collin having cancer, it made you a little afraid, because you're having feelings for him. It would be challenging based on what you went through with Don, knowing you were being drawn to a man who could take you down the same road again."

Catherine shook her head. "No, I told you. We're just friends." She didn't sound convincing even to herself.

Genny closed the magazine. "Well, if you are, I'm a size two."

Catherine dropped an ornament back into the box. "You're right. I am having feelings, but I don't even know what to call them. For goodness sake, I've known him only a few days. I like being around him, and the kids love him. We have many of the same interests. But on the other side, there's the ever present Krysta, his agent who he used to date, and then finding out he also suffered from melanoma . . . It's like I'm weighing one side against the other."

"That doesn't sound like the Catherine I met when I first moved here. You know, the one I always said was absurdly optimistic."

88

Catherine smiled. She remembered. "I think somehow that girl got lost in all the grief."

Genny reached for a glass of water and took a sip. "Well, here's an opinion coming from a medical professional. I think you should find her, bring her back, and get out of your head about all this stuff. Let your heart have a chance."

Catherine lifted a mockingbird with a tiny heart on its side. She wondered why Agnes painted it that way. She turned the bird around for Genny to see.

"See?" Genny said. "Even the stuffed birds are agreeing with me. That bird always symbolized the love of my grandmother and grandfather. His favorite bird was a mockingbird."

Though he'd died young, in their conversations, Agnes often mentioned her late husband with great affection.

Catherine's cell phone buzzed in her pocket. Collin's name flashed on the screen.

"Hi, Collin. I thought you'd be snapping photos," she said.

"I'm about to go, but I wondered if I might say yes to your offer of using the SUV."

"I'm staying with Genny all day, so it's a perfect time. She lives across the street from me. Come on by and swap the cars." Although, she did detest the idea of seeing the Krysta-car in the yard all day.

"So he's coming here?" Genny asked after she hung up.

"Yes, and please be on your best behavior," Catherine said. In a few moments, the crunch of gravel signaled Collin's arrival. It didn't take long from Betty's Bed and Breakfast.

"Come in," Genny called.

Collin stepped through the door, looking handsome in jeans, boots, and a khaki shirt, with sunglasses on his head. He appeared ready for whatever adventure lie ahead. "How are you two doing today?" he said with a smile, holding out his keys.

"We're doing fine. You know David, but I'm not sure you and Genny have met. Genny, this is Collin. Collin, Genny."

"Forgive me for not getting up," Genny said. "These twins are calling the shots these days."

"You need to take care of them and you," Collin said. "It's great to meet you. David has gushed about you."

Genny smiled.

Catherine loved the way Genny and David were with each other, but she couldn't help but remember it wasn't always that way. Genny had been suspicious of David at first because of his involvement with the developer, who'd threatened to seize her property. But in time, she saw the good in him and was willing to take a chance.

She took Collin's keys and placed them on the table behind the sofa, then reached into her purse, grabbed her own, and handed them to him. "The gear shift sticks a little, so you have to be persuasive, but otherwise, it's fine."

"I know it will be. Looking forward to going to the river today. Hope to snag some great shots."

"Oh, I have to show you this." She led him over to the Christmas tree. "Look at what Genny's grandmother made." She pulled the RCW from a top branch. "Genny said Agnes liked to paint from her own photos, so she might have seen the RCWs, too."

She placed the bird in Collin's hand, and he held it to the light. "This is amazing. Wow, wouldn't these sell well at the mill?" He turned to Genny. "What would you think of allowing me to replicate these?"

"It's fine with me, and I think grandmother would love to share them with more people than me, David, and the babies." She pointed to her belly, not using any names because she and David were waiting until the birth to share them.

"Do you mind if I take photographs of them? And what was your grandmother's name?"

"No, go right ahead. Her name was Agnes Sanders."

"We could call it the Agnes Sanders Collection by Donnelly Designs. And the profits go to a habitat preservation foundation."

Genny smiled. "People in town would love to see her name on something like that. She was such a big supporter of the arts, and her paintings are spread far and wide."

Collin began angling for shots of the birds as they hung on the tree. He removed a few and placed them on a table so as not to miss any of the detail Agnes was careful to include.

He pointed to the mockingbird. "What's the heart here mean?"

Genny explained the symbolism.

"Oh," Collin said and took several shots of it. "Makes this one extra special." He stopped for a moment. "In fact, wouldn't it be great to include a story with each of these?"

Catherine nodded.

"It would, but I don't know much about the other birds," Genny said.

"We'll work on it," Collin said with confidence. He turned to Catherine. "I alerted the Fish and Wildlife Service about the RCW. They're going to get back to me. Of course, sometimes it can take a while. And if necessary, I can bring in the foundation I work with.."

"I did speak with Louvene, and she's checking into who might have bought the RCW property."

"Good deal," Collin said. "We should know something soon." He turned to go. "I'll give you a call when I'm finished to see where you are so I can return the car."

As the door closed behind Collin, Genny said, "Oh, my."

"What, a pain or something?"

"No, not at all. It's the way you two gaze at each other."

"No, we don't gaze at each other."

"Oh, yes you do."

Catherine shook her head and put another ornament on the tree.

TEN

Early Friday morning, after she'd returned from taking the kids to school, her phone rang. "Oh, hi, Louvene. How are you?"

"I'd be better if David Worth would clean off his desk. That man is a pack rat if I've ever seen one. It's worse than ever with those babies coming."

Genny could hear shuffling in the background, as if Louvene were trying to find something on David's desk.

"You'd think he'd want to get things in order before he takes off for a while. It's an embarrassment. Looks like I'm going to have to take care of it myself. Anyway, the reason I called is I found who bought the property you were interested in. It's a group called E and W Land Company. I was in kind of a hurry when I was at the courthouse, so I didn't get any further than that."

"Well, thank you. You've been a real help. And thanks for staying with Genny tomorrow."

"No problem at all. And I could do Tuesday and Thursday next week. David has court cases one of those days, and he is out of town the other. I can have the office phone forwarded to my cell."

"Great. Earlene Bouvier is also coming up with some names. I'll let her know. This is a big help."

"Glad to do it. Can't wait to put my hands on those little babies. All my grandchildren are grown."

Catherine imagined Louvene almost felt like the babies' grandmother, since she treated David like he was her son instead of her boss.

"We're all excited. Talk to you soon." She hung up. E and W Land Company. Shouldn't be too hard to find who the principles are.

Her watch indicated only one hour before a meeting with Collin at Connie's Coffee and Cones. He wanted to show her the photographs he took on his outing the day before, and she now had info for him, too.

The idea of him having cancer made her shudder and she tried to push the thought out of her mind. She needed more time to process this and didn't know whether to bring it up or not.

One hour gave her time to load the dishwasher and fold two baskets of clothes and put them away. When she drove into town, she spotted Collin's car near Connie's. A little tingle went through her at the thought of seeing him again. As she opened the front door, she found him at a table against the wall. Right under the, "There is a season" sign. She told herself it was a coincidence.

Collin sitting under the sign wasn't a "sign." That song about how this was the most amazing season of the year wafted from the speakers in the shop, making the place seem extra festive. She ordered a latte from Sofia and slid into a seat.

"You won't believe what I found by the river," he said without even greeting her. He turned his computer for her to see.

Long slender legs, gray body, red crown. "A sandhill crane," she cried. "Could it be the same one I'd seen in my backyard?"

"I wondered the same thing. He might have stopped off in this area for a while to refuel before going a little farther south."

Sofia delivered her latte, and Catherine took a sip of the soothing beverage. What were the odds they'd see the same bird, one rarely observed in this part of the state? She scrolled through the pictures Collin took and was awed at all he'd captured.

She came to a photo of a painting featuring a gray-bodied bird with a flashy red cap. He was depicted with a bow tie and glasses. "Did you do this?"

"I did. A preliminary sketch of the sandhill crane. I think I would call him Elbert. He's a professor."

"Incredible. You are talented."

"Thanks," he said. "I have big plans for Elbert. He's going to help kids learn a lot about birds."

"I'm sure he will." Catherine loved Collin's imagination. She was smitten by his artistic ability and how he could spin a bird sighting into something so cute that could be used for good that she almost forgot about her news. "Oh, and I need to tell you . . . I heard from Louvene. The land where the RCWs are was purchased by E and W Land Company. We don't know the principles, but I'll work on that."

"Sounds good, and I'll let you know if I hear from the Fish and Wildlife people."

Just as she was getting ready to ask him about the cancer, a buzz sounded from Collin's pocket. He pulled his phone out and checked the caller ID. "Please excuse me, I was expecting this call." He pressed it on, rose from his seat, and walked toward the front of the shop.

Drifts of the conversation drifted back to Catherine. "Three book . . ." and "next week . . ." After a few minutes, Collin returned, his eyes wide, brow furrowed as if he were bewildered. He dropped into his seat.

"What is it?"

"It's amazing . . . crazy."

Adrenaline rose in her, and she leaned forward. "Who was it? What did they say?"

"It was Krysta. She texted earlier that she had news for me."

In a moment, the adrenaline rush reversed, and a sense of dread came over her. She sat back in her seat.

"She thinks she may have landed a deal with a big publisher for a series of books. They want to buy the rights for my current book from the small publisher I'm with, and they're thinking about starting with three others and see how they sell. These would be books for other states in the southeast similar to the *Georgia Birds and Their Stories* book. Based on sales of my current book, they are optimistic."

"That's great news," she said, trying to be excited for him.

"It is . . ." He paused. "But she says they want to meet with me next Wednesday. In Chicago."

Catherine swallowed. "A Chicago company wants to publish books about the Southeast?"

"Yeah, the publishing world is crazy."

"Next week, then?" She stirred her coffee and lowered her head, trying to keep her disappointment from showing. Just when the door of her heart cracked open the tiniest bit, he would be gone. She bit the inside of her lip.

"Right. It's moving pretty fast. Krysta will go with me to negotiate the deal. We'll fly to Chicago on Tuesday, have meetings on Wednesday, and then return Thursday."

Yippee. Overnight stays in another city with Krysta in the next room. She hated how she was so suspicious of her.

"You okay?" Collin asked.

"I'm fine." She collected herself, put on her game face, and forced a smile. "This is a huge opportunity." She couldn't let him see this ugliness in her. This was a big opportunity to do good, to make others aware of the plight of birds.

"It is." He turned his gaze toward the window, and his eyes glassed over as if he were peering into the future. "It's a dream come true," he said. "What I've been working toward for a long time. It's an opportunity to educate children at young ages about the birds that fill their skies with calls and song."

How could she have one ill feeling about him pursuing this book deal simply because Krysta was going along?

"I have to let Betty at Betty's Bed and Breakfast know I'll be leaving tomorrow. I need to return to Atlanta to prepare and think through a plan for which states might come first. This is going to take some time."

She imagined he did have much work in front of him. She directed her gaze to him. "I wish you the best," she said.

He reached over and took her hands. "That means a lot. I sure will miss Worthville, and . . . you."

The warmth of his hands was so soothing. "I'll miss you, too."

"Let's keep in contact about the RCW, though. And let me know how Genny is doing?"

"Will do," she said. Was he going to say something definite about seeing her when he returned? After all, David did say Collin thought of their relationship as more than friends. Oh, how she wished he would.

He picked up his camera and rose from his chair. "I'll call you." He leaned over and hugged her. "We'll be in touch."

We'll be in touch. That sounded like something you'd say to a business colleague. Maybe he'd changed his mind about them. He strode toward the door, and as she watched him step onto the sidewalk and head toward his car, another Christmas song chimed on about it feeling like Christmas.

She wasn't sure it did.

❄

After he left, Catherine spent the next few days wrapping Christmas presents, baking cookies, and generally trying to get her mind off the situation. At least her Christmas preparation was better than years before. She tied a big multicolored bow on the present she'd gotten for the twins—his and hers mobiles for the crib. But really, they could be interchangeable, the dangling bears or lambs would entertain either child. She and Genny had talked a couple of times, but she waited until the next Wednesday when she was scheduled to stay with her to unload the whole story.

Shortly after she arrived at Genny's and told her what was happening, Genny asked, "He's in Chicago right now with Krysta?"

Catherine plopped in a chair and nodded. "Yep, for three days. They flew to Chicago yesterday, have meetings today, and because they weren't sure how long it would take, didn't schedule their return until tomorrow."

Genny rubbed her stomach and tried to straighten a kaftan type thing she must have purchased online, because Catherine knew she hadn't been shopping, and it appeared to be new. She imagined David's wardrobe had been exhausted. Those babies were growing so much, even the kaftan pulled at the seams.

"Have you heard from him?" Genny asked.

101

"He called me when he arrived at the hotel to say again how much he enjoyed visiting Worthville. He was in a room on the twentieth floor with a great view of the city."

Catherine imagined Chicago at Christmas was beautiful. She'd seen pictures of Millennium Park and the city's sparkling Christmas tree. Wouldn't it be great to shop along Michigan Avenue or maybe go ice-skating? Perhaps just the idea of going ice-skating seemed appealing rather than the actual skating. Catherine had never been in a rink, unless she counted sliding around on an ice-covered sidewalk once or twice.

"When he said he enjoyed visiting Worthville, maybe he also meant he enjoyed visiting you. If he wanted to be with Krysta, he would be. But he's not. I think you have to trust that." Genny moaned as she shifted on the sofa.

Genny was right. This was absurd. He did say he would miss her. That was something. She'd known the man such a short while and should not be concerned about any of this. But the truth was, she did care what was going on with him, and this was the first time she'd given a thought to anyone else since Don had died. Maybe she would feel better if Collin had said more about getting together when he returned.

"Even if I could come to terms with his cancer, I can't seem to get past Krysta." This green-eyed monster of jealousy kept hounding her.

They spent the rest of the morning watching reruns of an old mystery show Genny's Grandmother Agnes had loved. It was almost as if she were there watching the shows with them. That seemed a comfort right now. Around noon, she was in the kitchen preparing lunch for Genny when her phone rang. Collin.

She pressed it on. "Hi, Collin. How's it going?

"I got it. I signed for a three-book deal, and based on sales, they hope to continue with books covering the entire southeast."

"Great. I'm happy for you." A brown thrasher pecking around on the ground outside the kitchen window stopped and eyed her as if he, too, thought it was fabulous news. "This is going to help children all over the south care about birds from their earliest years. Who knows what good it might do?" She paused a minute. "Are you and Krysta having fun?" She tried to ask the question in a casual way.

"So far, it's been just business, but I think tonight we're going to the Winter Wonderfest. Should be fun." The phone went silent for a moment. "Krysta has done much to help me, and this book contract is but one example of that."

103

Catherine plopped in a chair and sat there with the phone in her hand, wondering what to say. Krysta's involvement in his life sounded non-negotiable.

"Well, I'm happy for this book deal. Congratulations. Listen, I'm trying to prepare Genny's lunch, so I need to go. We'll talk another time." She hung up and cringed as she added the hot sauce Genny had requested to go with her chicken salad. But she also cringed, wondering how she would ever come to terms with this thing with Krysta and Collin. There seemed to be only one way, and that was to say goodbye to Collin.

ELEVEN

If she couldn't deal with her feelings about Krysta, she'd need to stay away from Collin. That's just the way it had to be. She gripped the steering wheel as she pointed the car out of her driveway, and then as soon as she pulled onto the road, she made a quick turn into Genny's. *Good, Louvene is already there.*

She exited her car and rapped on the front door. Then she pushed it open. "Anybody here?"

"We're here," Genny called from the sofa. "And then some."

Catherine laughed as she entered, and Louvene emerged from the kitchen carrying a plate. "Oh, hi, Genny. Did you forget something from yesterday?"

"No, I wanted to know how to find the principles of the company you said bought the property on Fairview Road. I tried to do a little digging on the internet, but I didn't find anything."

"Oh, that's easy. I didn't have time to do it, and I forgot later on. Not like me. I think I'm excited about the babies coming." Louvene put the plate on the sofa table and took a pad from her purse. She jotted a few words, tore a piece of paper from the pad, and handed it to Catherine.

Catherine nodded as she scanned the paper and read aloud. "Contact Worthville business licensing agency. Building adjacent to the courthouse." She slipped the paper into her pocket. "Looks pretty easy. Thanks. Oh, wait. I found diapers on sale. Let me run and get them."

Catherine came back in with the plastic package. "I hope y'all have fun this afternoon."

"We're going bowling today. Want to join us?" Genny said in a sarcastic way.

"Hold on, Mama, it won't be long until you're sending those balls down the lane," Catherine said. Genny had become quite a proficient bowler since she'd moved back to Worthville.

Genny rubbed her stomach as if doubting Catherine's words. "Maybe," she said. "I'm ready for these guys to make their appearance."

Catherine gestured to the plate Louvene had been carrying, "What is that?" She thought it might have been an omelet, but it smelled a bit strange.

"Oh, Genny requested an omelet, with cheese, onions, mushrooms . . ."

So far, all normal ingredients.

"And clams."

Catherine tried not to gag, said goodbye, and returned to her car. In a few minutes, when she parked at the courthouse, two buildings—not one—were adjacent to it. Fifty-fifty chance, she thought, and picked the one to the right. When she reached the front door, it read, "Worthville Business Licensing."

Hooray! She picked the right one. She entered, and a woman with red hair and porcelain skin greeted her. "Welcome, what can we help you with?"

How should she phrase it? The news she was in here checking on this company could travel fast. "I'm interested in a company that made a land purchase here. E and W Land Company. I'd like to contact them about a matter. Could you help me find the principles?"

"Sure," she said. She turned toward a computer. "We don't have the information posted online publicly, but I do have it in my computer." She made a few clicks. "I think this is the information you want." She turned the computer for Catherine to see.

Catherine read the info and then did a double-take. "Are you sure?"

"One hundred percent," she said.

Catherine exited the office with her hand over her mouth in shock. She didn't return to her car but made a left and kept walking. She passed the depot, then Connie's, and made another left turn into the bookstore.

She strode right to Tucker. "You own the property where the Red-cockaded Woodpeckers are?" Catherine blinked in astonishment as she studied Tucker's friendly face. She didn't wait for an answer. "Elijah Tucker and Winn Tucker are the principles in E and W Land Company. I can't believe it."

Everyone always called Tucker by his last name. Most people thought it was his given name.

"Believe it. Just closed on the property last Friday, my wife and I," Tucker said, straightening a stack of books on the counter by the cash register.

The door jingled as a customer came in and went straight for the local author section.

"We set up E and W Land Company as an investment. We'd heard about those woodpecker colonies over the years, and when we found the property for sale, we knew we must act to make sure it was protected for future generations. Plus, we've always wanted to have a little organic garden, and the roadside property in front is perfect for a smallish vegetable and flower garden."

This was the strangest turn of events. "I saw the surveyors out there, and Collin and I have been so concerned about who might be buying it. How did you know about the woodpeckers?" Catherine asked.

A man with a panicked look on his face burst through the door. "Where are the cookbooks?"

"Second stack on the right," Tucker said and then leaned over and whispered to Catherine. "I bet he's looking for that new Sarah Rose cookbook. Sold out last week. Can't get anymore."

Sure enough, the man reappeared. "The new Sarah Rose?" he asked.

"Sorry, we won't have any more until after Christmas."

The man's shoulders slumped, and he turned toward the door, then half turned back. "Do you have a replacement suggestion?"

Tucker gave him a big smile. "Check for the April Simmons cookbook. It's also popular if the person you're buying for doesn't already have it."

The man's face brightened as if he were a drowning man and someone threw him a life raft. "Thanks," he said.

Tucker focused on her again. "What was it you asked me? Oh, yes. How I learned about the RCWs. I believe Agnes Sanders, Genny's grandmother, was the one who told me about them. She'd been taking pictures of the countryside and spotted them. I told Genny's husband about the RCWs because of their proximity to the mill."

"And David told Collin because of his interest in birds. Those surveyors we ran into were acting on your behalf."

"Sorry for the scare."

"No problem. I'm glad there's a happy ending to this story." For the birds, at least. Happy endings for her seemed elusive.

Catherine went home, raked a few straggling leaves that she hadn't gotten around to, picked up the kids from school, and then reviewed her pantry supplies to see what she might have for dinner. After she put out the ingredients for tuna casserole, she checked her smart watch—4:45. Collin texted earlier that his plane was due into Atlanta from Chicago around five o'clock. She hoped to hear from him when he landed. Sure enough, her phone buzzed about thirty minutes later just as she set the oven to preheat.

"I'm on the moving sidewalk headed toward baggage claim," he said. "Glad to be back. Thought I'd come over to Worthville for a couple of days."

"I found out who bought the RCW land," she said, taking a casserole dish from the cabinet.

"Is it good news?"

"Well, yes, it is." She was glad the woodpeckers would be safe.

"Then don't tell me now. Tell me when I come. We can talk about it then. I need to go. I'm at the

escalator to the baggage claim. See you tomorrow."
He hung up.

She guessed it was just as well. She hated to tell
him her decision to break it off before he even
retrieved his bags from the trip. She opened a
pouch of tuna and poured it into a bowl.

Tomorrow would be a week before Christmas.
A part of her wanted to spend Christmas with
Collin and see where things would go, but she must
think of her kids. They were getting attached to
him, and wherever things went with their
relationship, Krysta would always be hovering. She
sighed.

When Collin arrived tomorrow, she would
need to put a period at the end of the sentence. Not
ellipses. A period.

A text came in Friday morning as she finished
adding birdseed to one of the feeders.

Collin: CAN WE MEET FOR COFFEE AT CONNIE'S?
10:00?

Catherine: SURE.

She put the bucket she used for the birdseed on
the ground and zipped her coat as the wind blew
the feeder. The weather had turned even colder.
When she checked the forecast on her phone, the

prediction for that weekend included snow. Rare for this part of Georgia.

When she arrived at Connie's, she sat, frozen, in her car. Not from cold weather but from dread. It filled her chest, making her heart pound. She hadn't even run her decision by Genny, who she was sure would try to talk her out of it. But what else could she do?

She entered Connie's where she was happy to see Sofia on duty. Connie would be sure to know something was wrong. She spotted Collin by the window, and he motioned for her to come over. She wouldn't be here long, so she skipped ordering anything.

He stood and gave her a hug, which she reciprocated. When she did, a part of her wanted to cling to him, but she resisted the urge and took a seat.

"You said you have good news?" he asked, swirling another peppermint latte.

"Good news? Oh, yes about the RCWs." She relayed the information about Tucker.

"How about that?" he said. "Tucker bought the property. Fabulous. I feel as if Tucker will allow us to go there anytime to see them. What a relief. They'll be protected. I'll let the Fish and Wildlife people know. They're overworked and will be happy for the good news."

She smiled and nodded.

He reached beside his chair. "I have a gift for you." He pushed a package in front of her. "I bought this for you in Chicago."

The package wrapped in red paper bore a glistening silver ribbon and screamed Christmas. "A Christmas present?" she asked.

"No, no, just something I saw that I thought you would like."

"Collin, I—"

He held up his hand. "It's nothing big." He gestured toward the present. "Open it."

She slipped the ribbon from the present and pulled back the paper. When she lifted the lid from the box and pushed back the tissue paper, she found a snow globe of an Eastern Bluebird. "It's beautiful," she said as she lifted it from the box and shook it, snowflakes swirling in the glass.

"I guess it's pretty cliché to bring someone a snow globe from Chicago, but I couldn't resist. I didn't realize that in the summer months, bluebirds are quite prevalent in Illinois, though they winter in the south."

"I love it," she said. "Thank you." She paused. "But Collin, I need to tell you something."

He took her hands. "You seem worried. What is it?"

"Do you remember what I said a couple of weeks ago about us being friends?'

He smiled. "I do, but—"

She shook her head to stop him from saying anything else. "No, I need to finish. I've made up my mind. I can sense our relationship might be moving toward something else, but just to be clear, we can only be friends. Nothing more."

He leaned forward. "But I want to—"

"It doesn't matter." She shook her head and took the snow globe. "Thank you for the gift. Have a nice Christmas." She headed toward the door and didn't look back, tears streaming down her face.

TWELVE

On the way home from meeting with Collin, Catherine stopped by Genny's. She looked in the rearview mirror and dabbed at her face with a tissue. Maybe no one would notice she'd been crying. Earlene opened the door. "Oh, Catherine, so good to see you. Come on in."

Catherine stepped in to find Genny propped up, drinking a smoothie of some sort.

"Have a seat Catherine. And since you're here, do you mind if I run upstairs, straighten up a bit, and put away the laundry?" Earlene asked.

"Not at all." Catherine eased into a wing chair.

Genny had been sleeping on the sofa downstairs for some time, so Catherine was sure, with Genny's size, she had not seen the upstairs in days or even weeks.

Catherine pointed to the smoothie. "Let me guess? Pineapple, horseradish, kumquat smoothie?"

"No, silly, everybody knows you have to add hot peppers."

Catherine wondered what the appetites of these two innocent babies would be like. They might come out of the womb demanding hot sauce in their milk.

"I need to tell you something." Her muscles grew rigid. "I severed ties with Collin.," she said, spitting out the words and bracing for the reaction

Genny's eyes widened, and she put the smoothie on a table. "You didn't?"

"I did, and I think it's the right decision." Catherine sat back in her chair. "In fact, there didn't seem to be any other way to go."

Genny reclined on the sofa, fanning herself with a magazine. "The right decision? I think you're not seeing clearly." Genny often spoke her mind, but being pregnant seemed to have given her an even greater sense of entitlement to say what she was thinking.

"You're blowing this up before it even has a chance," Genny continued.

Catherine crossed her arms. "It's better to do it now rather than everyone be hurt in a greater way later." Wasn't that true?

"It's almost as if you think the hurt is inevitable. Do you think that?" Genny held her hands out.

She didn't know. Maybe she did. "Anyway, I also stopped by to let you know I found who

116

bought the Red-cockaded Woodpecker land—Tucker and his wife, Winn. They wanted to protect the woodpeckers and use the front property for an organic garden."

Genny smiled. "That's great. The birds will be safe now. Good to know." She picked up the smoothie again and took a sip, apparently giving up on the business with Collin, for now at least.

"And the way he knew about the birds to begin with was your grandmother. She used to photograph them. I guess that's why she painted the RCW ornament."

Genny burst into tears. "I miss my grandmother so much."

Catherine rushed to Genny's side and knelt beside the sofa. "I'm sorry. I didn't mean to upset you."

"I wish she and my parents could have been here to see the babies." Genny's cheeks glistened with moisture.

"But we're all here. You have many friends in Worthville that love you." Catherine stroked Genny's hair. "Can I get you anything?"

"Well . . . maybe a peanut butter and mayonnaise sandwich?"

Catherine tried not to shudder. "Whatever you want."

The next morning, while her kids lounged on the sofa and watched a Saturday morning rerun of one of their favorite kid shows, Catherine sat at the kitchen table and stared out the window at darkening clouds. Apt symbols of how she felt. Heavy. Gloomy.

She went over everything in her mind again as she pulled her Bible toward her and opened to a place she'd bookmarked. That verse in Ecclesiastes kept coming back to her. "There is a time for everything and a season for every activity under the heavens."

She read on "A time to be born and a time to die, a time to plant and a time to uproot, a time to kill and a time to heal, a time to tear down and a time to build, a time to weep and a time to laugh, a time to mourn and a time to dance . . ." She rose and pressed her face to the window. "A time to mourn and a time to dance."

She'd done her share of mourning, but it had been a long time since she'd believed she would ever dance again.

The devotion about hanging on to a season in your life also cycled into her brain. Did she allow her jealousy of Krysta to grow so large in her head that she used it as a wedge between her and Collin so she wouldn't have to face uncertainty? After all, the familiarity of the past, even as hard as it was, could sometimes be less scary than allowing herself to be vulnerable.

She had to admit, that's exactly what she did. Genny was right. She hadn't been seeing clearly.

And maybe Collin was due a new season, too. After battling cancer, anyone would be. If she was afraid to have a relationship with him because of the cancer, it was like punishing him for being a survivor. If she were honest, she used his illness to push him away, as well.

Should she tell Collin how she felt? How she *really* felt instead of shoving off and not even giving them a chance?

She knew she had to, but before she did that, she needed to do something else. She stepped beyond the kid's eyesight, bowed her head, and whispered, "Lord, I don't want to be stuck in my grief. I asked You to help me, that I was tired of being the way I was, but I know I have to be willing for You to do that, so please help me to be open to a new season. Give me the clear vision I need in order to move forward. And help me to dance." She said an amen in her heart.

Would Collin even want to hear from her? She had to seem a little off with her back and forth behavior. Despite her reservations, she pulled out her phone and texted him.

Catherine: I'M SORRY ABOUT YESTERDAY. COULD WE TALK?

Collin: I'M STILL IN TOWN. HAD ALREADY BOOKED AT BETTY'S. I'LL COME TO YOUR HOUSE.

Catherine: SOUNDS GOOD.

Earlier in the week, she'd made cookies and stored them in a plastic container. Now, they caught her eye. She opened the top as quietly as she could so the kids wouldn't hear and snuck a couple out. If the kids heard, they'd demand cookies themselves. She hid in an adjacent room. Somehow, she thought the cookies might give her courage. Made her feel a bit like a hypocrite eating chocolate chips this early in the morning, but she did it anyway and brushed crumbs off her clothes. The kids were none the wiser.

When Collin arrived, the kids greeted him and showed him the Christmas presents under the tree. "They're not for us," John said. "Ours don't come until Christmas Day."

"Why, you folks are extra generous with all those presents you're giving away."

Lauren smiled as if she had purchased them all herself. Catherine was thankful she'd been able to finish her shopping with a week to spare. She was concerned Genny might go into labor any time, and then Catherine would be preoccupied with helping with the babies.

"Listen, kids. Mr. Collin and I need to discuss something. Could you two watch one more show while we do?"

120

Lauren and John, whose television watching was usually limited, bobbed their heads with energy, eyes wide.

Catherine helped them settle in and then motioned for Collin to join her on a garden bench just outside the back door where she could still keep an eye on the kids.

After they took a seat, Catherine opened her mouth to speak, but Collin interrupted. "Catherine, I didn't have a chance to say something yesterday. I was going to call you tonight." He took her hand in his. "I have sensed your reservation about Krysta, so I want you to know this— Krysta and I have come to an understanding. She will receive her percentage from all the books in the Chicago deal, but from this point forward, I am going with another agent in her company. I think she understood moving past our history was too hard if we worked together all the time. We agreed, for both of our sakes, to part ways."

The moisture welled in her eyes. "I was going to tell you I think I've used Krysta as an excuse to keep you away. I was still clinging to the past and afraid of getting hurt." The tears spilled over her cheeks. "And Collin?"

"Yes . . ." His compassionate eyes gazed into hers.

"David told me about your cancer, the melanoma." She paused, took a breath, and looked down for a moment. Then she lifted her gaze to his. "It's the same thing that Don died from."

He exhaled and shook his head. "What are the odds? I guess that scared you, didn't it?"

She nodded. "It scared me a lot."

He took her hands and squeezed them. "The doctors say I'm cured. Completely cancer free. But Catherine, none of us have a guarantee."

"I know. I accept that."

Collin pulled her close. "Remember what I said about wanting to save beautiful things?"

She nodded.

"Well, I believe we could have something truly beautiful. Let's try, okay? Let's try to save this. Let's allow this to be a new season in both of our lives."

"A new season," she said as he turned her face toward his and kissed her. She pulled away and stared into his eyes, and as she did, crystalline flakes drifted around them. "Snow," she said. "I can't believe it. It's magical."

"Yes, it is," he said, continuing to stare at her and pulling her back to him.

"Are you going to get that?" he asked.

"What?" she said, becoming aware of the buzzing in her pocket. She removed her phone and checked the caller ID. "Genny," she said. "Could be the babies. She pressed it on.

"We're on the way to the hospital," David said. "Have to go."

"I'll see you there," she said, hoping he heard her before hanging up. "This is still about a month early for the babies. Let's pray Genny and the babies will be okay."

Before she could say anything else, Collin grabbed her hands, dropped his head, and said, "Oh, Lord, watch over our friend Genny and these new little ones coming into the world. Thank You for keeping them in your care. In Jesus's name."

"Amen," Catherine said in agreement as warmth rose in her. "I'll call Earlene Bouvier to stay with the kids."

"You go. I'll stay until she gets here. I'll see you at the hospital later," Collin said. She watched as he went back into the house. She dialed Earlene and arranged for her to come. As she hung up, the kids came streaming from inside.

"Snow! Snow! Why didn't you tell us?" John said, spinning in the swirling flakes.

"Yeah, Mom, this is amazing," Lauren said, sticking out her tongue trying to catch one.

"Listen, kids, Collin will be here a few minutes until Mrs. Bouvier comes over to stay with y'all while I go to the hospital. Genny is having her babies tonight."

Lauren became still and clasped her hands together. "Snow and babies in one night. It's a dream come true," she said.

"It certainly is," Catherine said. Collin winked at her.

Catherine zipped to the hospital, and after a friendly volunteer directed her to the right waiting room, she took a seat in a green vinyl chair. She brought a book with her, but no way would she be able to concentrate.

A television in the corner of the room was tuned to the twenty-four-hour weather station, which showed a map of Georgia with areas of snow covering much of the northern half. "So it looks like if you kids have been wishing for a white Christmas, we're giving you a little touch of it a week before," the announcer said.

As she sat there waiting for any kind of news, other friends of Genny's drifted in. In only a couple of hours, it seemed half of Worthville stood outside the window where the babies were. The twins wasted no time in making their arrival. Tucker, his wife, Winn, Connie and her husband Michael, Louvene, and others gathered with noses pressed against the window. Collin arrived and slipped in beside her.

"Hi," she said.

"Hi, yourself," he replied.

"There they are," she said, pointing to the babies. She repeated what David had told them when he announced their arrival. "The girl is Agnes, after Genny's grandmother, and the boy is

124

named Benjamin, after David's ancestor who started the mill."

"They're cute," Collin said.

"Very," Catherine agreed.

Out of her peripheral vision, she could sense him scanning the crowd around them.

"Remember what I said about liking that the RCWs are social and live in groups?" he asked.

"Yes."

He pointed to a hallway a few feet from the window, and they stepped toward it, away from the group.

"Well," he pointed to the people at the window and then to her, "I like this group here and want to make my home in Worthville, too. I'm tired of the big city. What do you think about me moving here?"

"Really?" Her heart leaped to her throat, and she tried to tamp her excitement by swallowing hard. Before she knew what she was doing, she kissed him and didn't care who saw them.

The inevitable "oohs" and "ahhs" rose from the crowd at the window. Collin laughed, wrapped his arms around her, and held her tight. And then, right there in the hospital corridor, they began to sway, dancing to a song coming through the speakers overhead.

About thirty minutes later, David ushered her back to see Genny.

"The babies are amazing," she said as she sat beside Genny's bed.

"Aren't they beautiful?" The expression on Genny's face conveyed the depths of her gratitude and the hopes of their future.

"They are."

Genny frowned a bit and studied her. "What's going on with you?"

An uncontainable smile broke out on Catherine's face. "The doctor was right, as she usually is."

"Collin?"

Catherine nodded.

Genny reached over and touched her face. "I'm so glad. It's time for a little joy."

"That's what we thought."

THIRTEEN

O n Christmas eve, Catherine thought the kids were going to come out of their skin, they were so excited. John had already knocked several ornaments off the tree during one of his flying trips through the house, pretending to be a reindeer, and Lauren had changed her clothes three times trying to decide on the exact outfit for their trip to the live nativity at Worthville Church.

"I want baby Jesus to see me," she said, wearing red striped leggings and a sparkly pink top.

"Just remember that the real Jesus sees you all the time," Catherine said. A knock sounded on the back door, and Catherine went to answer. "Come in," she said.

"Are you folks ready?" Collin asked.

"Almost," Catherine said, giving him a hug. "I'm shocked Betty had an opening for you tonight."

"Betty said there was always room for me in the Inn." Collin laughed. "She said I've become one of her favorite customers. Of course, that's going to change when I move here."

Catherine nodded. "I can't wait." Her phone buzzed in her pocket. David Worth flashed on the caller ID. She answered.

"Catherine, how are you?"

"We're a little wild over here but about to go to the church's live nativity. How's Genny and the babies?"

"Doing great. Genny fed the babies, and now she's eating sauerkraut and sardines for supper."

Catherine's stomach did a little flip. "Oh, no. I thought her food cravings would end once she had the babies."

"I'm afraid not. It looks like her bizarre appetite may be here to stay."

Catherine had no idea how they might do lunch in the future.

"I know it's Christmas Eve and all, but I wanted to run something by you. Genny said you were thinking of going back to work now that the kids are older."

Catherine glanced over at Lauren, who was helping John put on reindeer socks. She couldn't believe how big they were. "Yes, I think it's time."

"Would you consider taking over the management of the Mill? My law practice has really grown and so has the mill business. The retail operation is more than I can handle now."

Managing the mill. Getting to stay in that beautiful environment all day. She knew immediately what her answer was. "Yes, yes, I'd love to do that." She was at last going to use her business degree.

Collin stared at her, his eyes wide.

"We'll talk more next week and firm things up, but this is great news. Have a merry Christmas."

"Merry Christmas." Again, a smile spread across her face. Managing the mill. Getting to source all their wonderful products. When she thought about returning to work, she never imagined it would be in such a fun place.

"What is it?" Collin asked.

When she told him, he said, "Oh, does that mean you're going to try and get me down on my prices?"

She shook her head. "Not you because I know you contribute to the wildlife foundation. But I will get to work with you on the Agnes Sanders Collection, won't I? How fun is that?"

"That is a lot of fun." He took her in his arms, and as she nestled into his shoulder, she realized there really is a season for everything.

ABOUT THE AUTHOR

Award winning Southern writer, Beverly Varnado, is a novelist, screenwriter, and blogger who writes to give readers hope in the redemptive purposes of God.

She has written a nonfiction memoir as well as several novels and screenplays, one of which was a finalist for the prestigious Kairos Prize in Screenwriting. The novella, *A Season for Everything*, is the third work in a series set in Worthville, Georgia. Previous novels set there are *A Key to Everything* and *A Plan for Everything*. Her work is also included in several anthologies and periodicals. As an artist, her work was recently chosen for exhibit at a state university gallery.

She lives in Georgia with her husband, Jerry, and their chocolate Aussiedor who is outnumbered by several cats. Beverly is *Mom* to three children and *Mimi* to two grandchildren.

Read her weekly blog *One Ringing Bell*, peals of words on faith, living, writing, and art at

oneringingbell.blogspot.com.

www.BeverlyVarnado.com
https://www.facebook.com/BeverlyVarnadoAuthor
Twitter @VarnadoBeverly
Beverly Varnado on Instagram.